Ink & Embers

Sophia Newman

Ink & Embers

A Novel by Sophia Newman

This is a work of fiction. Names, characters, places, and incidents are the product of the author's imagination or are used fictitiously. Any resemblance to actual events, locales, or persons, living or dead, is entirely coincidental.

First Edition: September 2025

Cover Design by: The Author

Printed in USA

ISBN: 978-1-997668-48-0

Chapters

Acknowledgments & AI Use Disclaimer

This book was shaped not only by long walks, late nights, and too many cups of tea—but also by the thoughtful support of tools that helped bring clarity, structure, and rhythm to the writing process.

I would like to acknowledge the use of AI-assisted tools, including OpenAI's ChatGPT, which supported the development of this novel in the following ways:

- Assisting with story outlining and structural planning
- Aiding in editing and continuity checks
- Supporting research and formatting during the drafting process

While every word, voice, and emotional arc belongs to the characters and their imagined world, the tools used behind the scenes were part of a collaborative and creative workflow— never a replacement for the heart of the story, but a quiet companion in building it.

The author retains full creative ownership of the characters, dialogue, plot, and emotional themes found within *Ink & Embers*.

This novel is a work of fiction. Any resemblance to real persons, living or dead, is purely coincidental.

With gratitude for the tools that help us tell quieter stories louder—and for the readers who give them a place to land.

~ Sophia Newman

Inbox Inferno

There was a special kind of despair that came from reading the fifth bad manuscript in a row before 10 a.m., and Harper Quinn had mastered the art of hiding it behind a well-practiced smirk.

Her office was a glass-walled cube tucked in the corner of the Quinn Literary Agency's Manhattan floor, a place that had once buzzed with industry energy and midlist optimism. Now, it hummed with a different tone—a low-grade anxiety masked by pressed suits, silent glances, and too much coffee. The glory days of print were over. Digital was king, TikTok sold more books than award committees, and Harper was barely keeping her clients, and her agency, afloat.

She stared at her screen, where a blinking cursor hovered over the opening line of yet another debut novel that promised to be "genre-shattering." The line read: *"The vampires weren't supposed to sparkle—but neither were they supposed to tap dance."*

Harper rubbed the bridge of her nose. "Make it stop," she muttered to no one.

Behind her, Simone—her relentlessly optimistic assistant— poked her head in, holding a triple-shot oat milk latte like a peace offering.

"Thought you might need this," Simone said, her eyes darting between Harper and the unread inbox counter ticking past 89.

"I needed a drink," Harper said dryly, taking the cup anyway. "But this will do."

"Rough morning?"

"I'm questioning the future of storytelling because a grown man just submitted a 350-page manuscript written entirely in rhyming couplets. About werewolves. In middle school."

Simone grimaced. "Yikes."

Harper leaned back in her chair, letting the bitter heat of the coffee anchor her back to reality. "It's like wading through literary quicksand. Every time I think I've found something solid, it turns out to be a cleverly disguised disaster. I swear, if I get one more email with the phrase 'the next Colleen Hoover,' I'm setting my desk on fire."

"Well, maybe the next one's it," Simone said brightly. "You never know."

Harper snorted. "That's the lie we tell ourselves."

She glanced toward the wall of framed book covers behind her desk—once-proud trophies of her early career. Ten years ago, Harper had been a rising star: a hungry twenty-something agent with a sharp eye for voice and a sharper tongue in contract negotiations. But hits had become harder to find, and risk-averse publishers were now more concerned with an author's social media presence than the actual prose.

She'd learned the hard way that passion didn't sell books anymore. Algorithms did.

Her phone rang, cutting through her thoughts.

Simone gestured. "Line two. Eleanor Chen."

Harper's hand froze halfway to the receiver.

Eleanor was the agency's founder. Once Harper's mentor. Now more like the godfather of a dwindling empire.

Harper picked up, already bracing herself.

"Harper Quinn."

"Ah, good. You're alive," Eleanor said, voice like aged whiskey—elegant but dangerous. "And hopefully not buried under a pile of werewolf erotica."

"Just middle-grade," Harper replied. "We're still safe for now."

"I won't waste your time. I have something you need to hear. A prospect."

Harper leaned forward. "A new client?"

"An old one. Elias Stone."

The name hit Harper like a physical jolt. She gripped the edge of her desk.

"No one's heard from him in ten years."

"Well, someone has now. Me."

Harper narrowed her eyes, instinctively skeptical. "Elias Stone is a ghost."

Eleanor's voice remained calm. "And ghosts are only dangerous if you stop believing in them."

"He disappeared after his wife died," Harper said, softer now. "Walked out of a publishing contract. Vanished. No one's even seen a grocery receipt."

"That's about to change. He's agreed to meet."

Harper blinked. "He *what*?"

"You'll be driving up to Maine tomorrow."

"Excuse me?"

"He lives alone in some oceanfront cottage. Doesn't do phones, doesn't check email. Apparently keeps chickens. You'll go in person."

Harper scoffed. "Why me?"

"Because you're flailing, darling. No offense. You've been paddling upstream in a leaky canoe since January. This could be the thing that turns it around—for both of us."

"This isn't a comeback, it's a suicide mission. I'm supposed to convince a hermit to write a novel when he hasn't touched a keyboard in a decade?"

"Yes. And I suspect he might listen to you."

Harper shook her head. "Eleanor, I'm a literary agent, not a therapist."

Eleanor was quiet for a moment. Then she said something that Harper hadn't expected—soft, precise, dangerous in its accuracy.

"Sometimes the truest stories are the ones we're afraid to tell."

The line went dead.

***

Harper sat frozen for several seconds before slowly hanging up the phone.

That sentence echoed in her chest like a bruise being pressed. She stood, went to the window, and stared out at the steel-gray sprawl of the city below. Cars blurred. Lights flickered. Her world—fast, loud, sharp—suddenly felt distant.

Elias Stone.

The literary recluse whose books had made her want to be an agent in the first place. *Cinderglow*, his last published novel, had sold five million copies and broken her heart. His words had been like embers—quiet but hot, glowing in the dark long after you turned the page.

And then he'd gone silent.

Harper pulled out her phone and searched his name. Same as always—an empty Wikipedia entry, a few dated interviews, nothing new. The industry had moved on, but part of her hadn't.

There had always been rumors. That he blamed himself for the fire. That the unpublished manuscript he'd been working on at the time was too personal. That he'd never write again.

Now she was being sent to revive him.

Why her?

She didn't have an answer. But she knew one thing.

She needed a win.

Badly.

She turned to Simone, who had returned with a stack of contracts and a look that said *I heard everything*.

"Clear my schedule for the week."

Simone raised an eyebrow. "You're really going?"

Harper grabbed her coat. "Apparently I'm chasing ghosts."

***

The drive from Manhattan to Bar Harbor took nearly eight hours, though Harper made it in six and a half, fueled by adrenaline, caffeine, and the undercurrent of anxious determination she hadn't felt since her first year in publishing. She'd left at dawn, dodging early traffic and storms on the Connecticut turnpike, her Audi humming with purpose. She hadn't taken time off in almost a year, not unless you counted dental surgery, which she didn't.

Now, with the skyline shrinking behind her, she found herself immersed in rural silence for the first time in what felt like forever. The road unfurled before her like a long sentence with no punctuation. Pine trees flanked either side of the narrow state highway, damp from recent rain. The farther she drove, the more the air changed—less exhaust, more salt.

Somewhere outside Portland, she started talking to herself.

"This is insane," she muttered. "Completely unhinged. Who does Eleanor think I am, some kind of literary priestess? Am I supposed to perform a resurrection?"

Still, she didn't turn around.

Instead, she fished through her glove compartment at a red light and pulled out a worn paperback: *Cinderglow*. The spine was cracked, the cover curled at the edges from too many subway rides. She'd carried this copy with her for years—half for nostalgia, half for something else she hadn't wanted to name.

Flipping to the first page, she read the opening line aloud, just to hear it again:

"There are silences that echo louder than screams."

It was Elias Stone at his finest—concise, poetic, devastating. The kind of line that made you want to put the book down and stare into space for a while. He had a gift for getting under your skin without trying.

She'd discovered *Cinderglow* in college, in a used bookstore wedged between a laundromat and a psychic on Canal Street. The shop had smelled like mildew and peppermint. She'd been broke and heartbroken from her first serious breakup, dragging herself through a semester of classes and ramen dinners, when that book called to her from a crooked shelf like some battered lighthouse.

It had wrecked her.

The story—about a grieving father raising his daughter after his wife's sudden death—wasn't flashy or high-concept. But it was honest. Raw. There was a tenderness between the lines, a heartbreak so quietly handled that Harper felt seen in a way no therapist, parent, or professor had ever managed. Elias Stone hadn't written characters—he'd written people.

And then, just when his career was about to catapult into literary stardom, he vanished.

No fourth book. No press. No closure.

The romantic in her—long buried under cynicism and deal memos—had always believed his silence had meaning. That some books demanded more from their authors than anyone realized.

Now, somehow, she was going to ask him to speak again.

As she crossed into Mount Desert Island, a fog began to roll in off the water, curling across the road in pale ribbons. The GPS stuttered. Signal gone. Harper wasn't surprised. Eleanor had said he lived off the grid—almost literally. No cell reception, no email, no assistant. Just a name on a mailbox at the end of a winding private road.

When she finally reached the turnoff, the forest grew denser. The trees arched above her, branches knitted like fingers holding secrets. Her tires crunched along a gravel path that twisted through the woods until it opened onto a clearing overlooking the ocean.

The cottage was two stories of salt-worn wood and rough stone, tucked into a cliffside like it had been there for a century. A small greenhouse sat to one side, partly overgrown. Chickens pecked at the dirt near a sloping garden, and from the chimney, a thin line of smoke curled upward into the overcast sky.

It looked exactly like the kind of place someone would go to disappear.

Harper parked and turned off the engine. For a moment, all she heard was the ticking of the car as it cooled, and the distant hiss of waves hitting rock.

She got out and walked up the path, boots slipping slightly in the mud. On the porch, she knocked twice, firm and professional.

No answer.

She tried again.

Still nothing.

She was about to call out when the door opened—just a crack—and a face appeared behind it.

Elias Stone looked older than his book-jacket photo, naturally. Time had drawn lines across his face and added streaks of silver to his unkempt hair. But it hadn't softened him.

His eyes were sharp. Guarded. Blue like winter glass. He wore a faded green sweater and worn jeans. No shoes.

He looked like a man who hadn't spoken to anyone in weeks—and wasn't particularly eager to start.

"You're late," he said, voice low and rough around the edges.

Harper blinked. "The GPS went dead."

"I told Eleanor I don't do visitors."

"And yet," she said, stepping onto the porch fully, "here I am."

He opened the door just enough to gesture for her to enter, then turned and walked away without another word.

So this is how it's going to be, she thought.

Inside, the house smelled like cedar and old books. The entry opened into a living room lined with shelves, every wall stuffed with novels and papers. A fireplace crackled quietly on the far side. The furniture was lived-in but clean. A mug sat on the coffee table, half full of dark tea. A heavy journal rested beside it, closed.

She stood just inside the doorway, uncertain.

"I wasn't expecting you until tomorrow," Elias said, disappearing into a side room. "Or at all."

Harper followed, slowly. "Change of plans."

"You didn't call."

"You don't answer."

He returned holding a second mug, which he handed to her with a grunt. "Tea. No milk. No sugar. I'm not a hotel."

Harper took it, impressed in spite of herself. "Noted."

He sat down in a leather armchair by the fire, gesturing loosely to the worn couch opposite. She sat carefully, taking in the view from the large window behind him—waves crashing against jagged stone, gulls circling like punctuation marks in the fog.

"You came to talk me into writing again," Elias said flatly, as if reciting a script he'd already decided he didn't like.

"I came to have a conversation," she said. "Whether that includes writing is up to you."

He eyed her. "You don't strike me as the patient type."

"I'm not. But I'm also not stupid."

He arched an eyebrow. "Debatable."

Harper smiled despite herself.

And in that moment—brief, flickering, electric—something shifted.

***

Harper took a sip of the tea. It was strong and a little bitter—like its maker.

Elias leaned back in his chair, hands steepled across his lap, eyes on the fire rather than her. It wasn't rudeness, exactly. More like detachment. As if he were studying a scene he'd seen a hundred times before and still didn't care for the ending.

"I didn't agree to write anything," he said at last, the flames casting his face in flickering amber. "I said I'd talk."

"That's all I'm here for," Harper replied. "Talking."

He turned toward her then, gaze cutting like a whetted knife. "You don't strike me as someone who wastes time with words unless they're going to be printed, bound, and slapped with a marketing campaign."

She smiled thinly. "That's fair. I'm not in the business of wasting time. But I'm also not in the business of pushing a man off a cliff just to make a headline."

"Really? That's refreshing. Most people in publishing would light the match if they thought it would sell an extra five thousand copies."

Harper's voice stayed even. "And you'd know, wouldn't you? You were their golden boy."

He flinched—not visibly, but Harper noticed the tiny shift in his posture. As if her words had pushed against a locked door he preferred stayed shut.

"I was never anyone's anything," he said quietly. "I wrote books. People bought them. That's the extent of it."

"You wrote books that *mattered*," she said, leaning forward. "That moved people. Don't pretend you don't know that."

He stood, abruptly, and walked to the window. Outside, the wind had picked up. The sea was darker now, slate and violent. Waves battered the rocky cliffs below. His silhouette, framed against the storm-glassed pane, looked every bit the myth he had become.

"That was a long time ago."

"Doesn't make it less true."

Elias crossed his arms. "You didn't come here to flatter me. What do you really want?"

Harper took a slow breath. This was the pivot point. She could lie, dress it up in agency spin and market talk. But she'd already sensed that Elias would see straight through it.

"I want a book," she said simply. "But more than that, I want to know why you stopped. You don't owe the world anything—but I think you owe yourself something."

He turned toward her, frowning. "And what would that be?"

"Closure. Truth. Peace. Call it whatever you want." She met his eyes. "You left something unfinished. That kind of silence doesn't just fade. It festers."

For a long moment, he didn't speak.

Then he moved to the fireplace, poked at the burning logs with an iron rod, and said in a quiet voice, "What do you know about fire, Ms. Quinn?"

Harper tilted her head. "Literal or metaphorical?"

"Either."

She thought for a moment. "It consumes. It changes the shape of everything it touches. And it leaves a scar that never fully goes away."

He nodded once. "Then maybe you understand more than I expected."

She wanted to ask him about the fire. The real one. The one that had taken his wife and turned his life into ash. But the moment didn't feel right. Not yet. There was too much in his voice still laced with smoke.

Instead, she changed tack.

"Let's talk about what you *would* be willing to write," she offered. "No pressure. No deadlines. Just... possibilities."

Elias chuckled darkly. "I haven't written a sentence in years. I barely keep a grocery list."

"But do you *want* to?"

He didn't answer right away.

Harper leaned forward. "Look, I'll be honest. I didn't come here to badger you into signing a contract. I came because I've read *Cinderglow* at least six times, and every single time I finish it, I want to crawl out of my skin. Because it *knows* something about grief that most writers fake."

Elias turned, slowly. "You think I faked it?"

"No. I think it was the most honest thing I've ever read. Which is probably why you haven't written since."

His eyes narrowed. "Careful."

She shrugged. "I'm not trying to be cruel. I'm trying to connect. You write like someone who's survived something. And people like that don't forget how to write. They just forget how to give themselves permission."

Silence stretched between them again, heavier now.

Harper set her tea down. "I brought some of your old notes. From your last editor. Things you left behind after the accident. I thought maybe—"

"I don't want them."

"Maybe not. But you might want what's *in* them."

He walked past her and opened a cabinet by the fireplace. Inside was a small record player and a neatly stacked collection of vinyl albums. He pulled one out—Miles Davis—and placed the needle.

Soft jazz poured through the space, filling it with something that felt like memory.

"Do you know what it's like to lose the only person who ever saw you?" he asked, voice so low it almost disappeared beneath the saxophone.

13

Harper didn't answer.

He turned to her.

"I do. So forgive me if I don't jump at the chance to open that wound just because the industry misses my prose."

Harper stood slowly. She didn't want to push further today. Not yet. But she didn't want to leave him unchallenged either.

"I'm sorry for what you lost," she said. "I really am. But I think somewhere in all that pain, there's still a story that only *you* can tell. And if you ever want to tell it—even just part of it—I'll be here."

Elias watched her quietly.

"Where are you staying?" he asked, finally.

"There's a little inn down in town. The Fog & Fern."

"It's half-rotted and overpriced."

"Sounds charming."

He didn't smile, but she thought his mouth twitched.

"Come back tomorrow," he said at last.

Then, with a nod so small she almost missed it, he turned and walked down the hall.

Harper stood there for another moment, Miles Davis whispering in her ears, the fireplace warming her back.

Then she picked up her bag, let herself out, and stepped into the wind.

She had no idea what tomorrow would bring.

But for the first time in a long time, she felt like she was on the edge of something real.

***

14

The Fog & Fern Inn sat just off the main street of Bar Harbor, nestled between a small antique bookstore and a shuttered ice cream parlor. The sign swung from a wrought iron hook, creaking gently in the evening wind. Warm light glowed from its windows, promising comfort—or at least functioning heat and a bed.

Harper pulled her suitcase from the trunk, legs stiff from the drive and her nerves still jangling from the encounter with Elias. She'd gone into that meeting prepared for indifference, even hostility. But she hadn't expected the *weight* of him. The grief, the intellect, the bitterness all coiled behind his sharp blue eyes like a storm with no exit.

She stepped inside the inn. The lobby smelled like lavender and old paper. A grandfather clock ticked in the corner, the kind that looked like it had a story to tell if you listened closely enough.

The innkeeper—a soft-spoken woman named Irene with wiry white hair and a cardigan three sizes too big—welcomed her with a polite smile and handed over a key attached to a piece of driftwood.

"Room three," Irene said. "Second floor, ocean view. Breakfast is at seven. You're here on vacation?"

Harper gave her the standard polite lie. "A little work, a little escape."

Irene nodded like she understood. "Most people who come here are running from something. Or toward it."

Harper's mouth quirked. "What if it's both?"

"Then you're in the right place."

She climbed the narrow staircase to her room, opened the door, and was greeted by the quiet comfort of simplicity: a double bed with a patchwork quilt, a writing desk by the window, and a view of the gray-blue sea where gulls skimmed the waves like scribbled notes on water.

She dropped her bag and collapsed onto the bed, staring up at the ceiling.

The room was still, but her mind was racing. That conversation with Elias had unsettled something inside her, something she hadn't felt in years—not just professional curiosity, but a pulse of... possibility. Of *purpose*.

She didn't want to admit how much she needed this trip.

The truth was, Harper wasn't just here to save her agency.

She was here to save herself.

The last eighteen months had been a brutal slide into burnout: two failed book launches, three major clients jumping ship, and one messy breakup with a fellow agent who'd decided that her ambition was "intimidating." Her confidence had frayed thread by thread, until she'd become a ghost of the woman who once swaggered into publisher meetings with a pitch and a plan and always walked out with a deal.

Now, she second-guessed everything. Every project. Every instinct.

And Elias Stone? He was her shot at redemption—not just for her career, but for her belief that stories still *mattered*.

She stood, poured herself a glass of water from the carafe on the dresser, and opened her laptop. No Wi-Fi. Of course not. Irene had said the router was down. "Storm damage," she'd muttered, which Harper suspected was just local code for *leave your tech and go outside.*

So she pulled out her leather notebook instead, the one she used for real notes—not contracts or numbers, but thoughts. Questions.

She flipped to a fresh page and wrote:

Elias Stone — Phase One: Access.

- Speaks in metaphors. Mistrusts publishers.
- Doesn't *want* to write. But might *need* to.
- Broken, but not unreachable.

She tapped the pen against her chin.

Then, with hesitation, she wrote:

What does *healing* sound like on the page?

The question made her chest ache a little.

She closed the notebook, walked to the window, and leaned against the frame.

Below, the harbor was dotted with boats tugging at their moorings, rocking gently against the current. It was the kind of scene that demanded quiet. That slowed your heart without asking.

She didn't want to sleep yet, but she didn't want to think too much either. So she changed into a sweatshirt, pulled the quilt over her legs, and let herself drift.

***

Back at the cottage, Elias sat by the fire, unmoving.

He hadn't lit the lamps. He didn't need them. The flames were enough.

He had expected her to be pushy. Slick. The kind of agent who used charm like a scalpel and praise like chloroform.

But Harper Quinn had surprised him.

She wasn't trying to flatter him. She wasn't even trying to manipulate him—at least, not in the way he'd assumed.

She spoke like someone who understood that stories weren't currency. They were confessions.

He got up, walked over to the old bookshelf by the wall, and pulled out a box from the bottom shelf. Inside were the remnants of a life left unfinished: journals, drafts, and one blackened folder that had once held the manuscript he'd abandoned the night of the fire.

He stared at it.

There were days he convinced himself he couldn't write again because the words had dried up.

But there were other days—like this one—when he feared the truth was worse.

That the words were still inside him.

And that they might burn him all over again.

***

The next morning, Harper woke to the scent of brewed coffee and something yeasty wafting up through the floorboards. Her phone was still out of service. No emails. No buzzing. No alarms. It was strange, disorienting, and oddly peaceful.

She dressed quickly, pulled her coat over her sweater, and headed downstairs. Irene greeted her with a plate of blueberry muffins and a French press on the table. The innkeeper slid into a seat across from her with a cat on her lap and a knowing smile.

"So, did you find what you were looking for?" she asked, voice light but not casual.

Harper considered lying again. But something about the woman's gaze—calm, weathered, a little witchy—made her answer honestly.

"Not yet," she said. "But I think I found someone who might have the map."

"Ah," Irene said, nodding slowly. "Then you'll stay a while."

Harper poured coffee into the mismatched ceramic mug and took a sip. It was good. Rich. Strong.

"Yeah," she said. "I think I will."

***

By late morning, Harper was back on the gravel road, driving through sunlight fractured by wind-stirred pine branches. The fog had lifted, replaced by clear, pale blue skies. The coastline sparkled in the distance, all jagged cliffs and silver foam.

She parked in front of Elias's cottage and cut the engine. For a moment, she sat with her hands on the steering wheel, breathing in the silence. She hadn't even realized until today how used she'd become to background noise—the churn of the subway, the clang of espresso machines, the constant hum of other people's ambition.

This quiet felt foreign. But not unpleasant.

The door to the cottage creaked open before she could knock.

Elias stood in the frame, squinting into the sun. He was wearing a flannel shirt over a faded black T-shirt and held a chipped mug in one hand. Coffee, probably. She was starting to suspect he lived almost entirely on caffeine, stubbornness, and memory.

"You're early," he said, not unkindly.

"I figured I'd startle you into cooperation."

He stepped aside without another word and let her in.

The fire was already lit. The scent of woodsmoke and something herbal—maybe sage—hung in the air. It felt warmer today, more alive somehow. As if the house had braced itself for company and then decided to tolerate it.

Harper took the seat across from his usual chair.

"So," she said, setting her notebook on the table between them. "Have we reached the grudging respect phase of our collaboration yet?"

"Too soon to tell," he said, taking a sip from his mug. "Ask me again when you stop using marketing lingo in conversation."

She grinned. "Fair enough."

He sat, but didn't immediately speak. Instead, he watched her with a thoughtful frown, like a puzzle he hadn't quite solved.

"You said something yesterday," he said. "That I haven't given myself permission to write again. What makes you so sure I ever wanted to?"

"Because you wouldn't have agreed to see me if you didn't."

He looked at her for a long moment. "You don't think I did it for Eleanor?"

"No," she said, voice calm. "You did it for you. You just haven't admitted it yet."

Elias exhaled through his nose, as if amused despite himself.

"I used to think writing could save people," he said finally. "That if I got the words right—if I captured something true—it would make the world less lonely."

"Did it?"

He paused. "For a while."

Harper nodded. "That's all any of us get, really."

She opened her notebook. "So, here's what I'm thinking. Forget the idea of a book, for now. No contracts. No deadlines. Just... writing. A scene. A paragraph. A line. We can brainstorm. See what shakes loose."

"I don't brainstorm."

"Fine. Then monologue."

Elias chuckled softly. "You're relentless."

She shrugged. "You knew what I was when you let me in."

He stood and crossed to a shelf near the back of the room. Pulled down a small black journal and tossed it on the table. It landed with a soft thud beside her notebook.

"I wrote something last year," he said. "Didn't show it to anyone. Wasn't meant to be anything."

Harper opened the journal slowly. The first page was covered in Elias's precise handwriting—sharp slashes, deliberate spacing. She read the first few lines silently, and her breath caught.

"There is a silence between grief and memory, a hollow that hums like an unfinished sentence. That's where I live now—in the pause."

She looked up. "Elias…"

"It's not a story," he said. "Just fragments."

"It's beautiful."

He didn't respond.

She turned another page. More entries. Some a paragraph long, others just a sentence. Snippets of thought, description, grief, aching honesty.

"You've been writing all along," she said quietly.

"I told myself it was just journaling."

"It's a draft. A voice. The beginning of something."

He leaned back, arms crossed. "I can't write about her."

Harper met his gaze. "Then don't. Not directly. Write *around* her. Let the story find its shape from what's missing."

A silence stretched between them again—this one less tense, more contemplative. The kind of silence that happened between two people realizing they might not be enemies after all.

"I brought a file," Harper said, reaching into her bag. "Eleanor gave me permission to share it. It's from your last editor—notes on your unfinished manuscript. Thought you might want to see where you left off."

22

Elias looked at the folder like it was something radioactive. "I burned most of that draft."

"I figured."

"But... not all of it."

She watched him closely. "What if we start with something new?"

His eyes narrowed. "You mean co-write?"

She raised an eyebrow. "Is that a no?"

"I don't collaborate."

"Then think of it as a challenge. I'll write a prompt. You respond."

Elias considered this, rubbing his jaw. "Why are you really doing this?"

Harper paused.

And for the first time since she'd arrived, she let the mask slip.

"Because I'm tired of pretending that any of this means something if it's not *real*. And your work—your voice—was the first thing in a long time that felt honest. If there's even a chance of helping you find that again, I have to try. Even if it goes nowhere."

Elias stared at her, expression unreadable.

Then he said, softly, "You talk like a writer."

Harper blinked. "I'm not."

"Maybe not yet."

For the first time, he reached across the table and opened the journal himself. Flipped a few pages. Stopped.

"This one," he said, tapping the page. "Read it."

Harper did. It was only four lines.

"She laughed once and it shattered something inside me.
I didn't know love could be loud.
I only knew how to whisper pain.
I think she heard me anyway."

She swallowed hard.

He was watching her carefully now. Not guarded. Just... open.

The quiet between them shifted again—no longer absence, but presence. A recognition. A thread beginning to tie itself between two lonely people neither of whom knew, just yet, how to hold the other end.

Harper closed the journal.

"Let's write," she said.

Elias nodded, slowly.

"Tomorrow."

***

That night, back in her room at the Fog & Fern, Harper stared at her ceiling and felt something unfamiliar pulsing beneath her ribs.

Hope.

A cautious, fragile thing.

But alive.

***

The Ghost Writer

When Harper arrived at Elias Stone's cottage the next morning, she was armed with two coffees, a yellow legal pad, and a stubborn refusal to let awkwardness dictate the day.

She wasn't sure why she'd brought the coffee. He hadn't asked for it, and she had no idea how he took it. Maybe it was a peace offering. Or maybe, if she were being honest, it was a small way of feeling normal—of bringing a familiar gesture into an unfamiliar world.

The door was already open when she pulled into the gravel drive. She stepped out of her car, the hem of her coat whipping in the brisk sea breeze. Gull cries echoed overhead, and somewhere to her left, the rhythmic rush of waves met the rocky shore.

Elias was on the porch, seated in a wicker chair, a weathered paperback in hand and a steaming mug on the railing beside him.

"Brought reinforcements," she said, holding out one of the coffees.

He eyed it like it might explode. "You don't strike me as the sharing type."

"I don't share manuscripts. Coffee is negotiable."

He hesitated, then reached out and took it. "What is it?"

"Black. No sugar. Thought I'd play the odds."

He took a sip. "Tolerable."

High praise, she thought.

"Ready to get started?" she asked, settling into the other chair.

Elias closed his book without marking the page—either he had it memorized, or he didn't care.

"Define 'started.'"

"You write. I read. We argue. Maybe something good happens."

He gave her a sidelong glance. "You enjoy conflict, don't you?"

She smiled. "I enjoy *clarity*."

"I see."

They sat in silence for a beat, both sipping, both studying the ocean like it might offer direction. Then Elias stood, motioning for her to follow.

"Come on. I'll show you the office."

Inside, the cottage was quiet and sun-dappled, the scent of cedar and sea salt lingering in the air. He led her down a narrow hallway past a closed door that she instinctively knew was off-limits. Then another. Then, finally, they reached a room at the end of the hall.

It was not what she expected.

No organized desk with color-coded tabs. No inspirational quotes. No laptop, no Wi-Fi router humming in the background.

Instead, the room was filled with light—filtered through gauzy curtains over wide windows that looked directly out at the ocean. A massive oak table dominated the center, strewn with paper, books, several pens, a battered typewriter, and a dusty jar of fountain ink. On the walls hung sketches—soft pencil renderings of cliffs, gulls, and open hands.

"Did you draw these?" she asked, moving toward one of the sketches.

Elias shrugged. "Keeps the fingers moving."

"They're beautiful."

He didn't answer. He walked to the table, cleared a spot with one sweep of his hand, and gestured to a nearby chair.

"This is where the ghosts live," he said. "If they want to speak today, they'll show up."

Harper pulled out the chair and sat, placing her pad on the table. "You always talk about writing like it's a séance."

"It is."

She paused, then grinned. "Do I need to bring a candle?"

"Only if you want to summon something."

They got to work.

Or rather—they *tried*.

Harper began with a simple prompt. "What if we wrote from the point of view of someone who *can't* tell the truth—not because they're lying, but because it would destroy the one person they love?"

Elias looked unimpressed. "Sounds like a soap opera."

"It's also the foundation of ninety percent of good literature."

He didn't argue that.

Still, the next hour was... slow.

Elias wrote in longhand, and not quickly. Harper occasionally paced the room, glancing out the windows or making notes on her pad. Every time she tried to offer suggestions, Elias would raise an eyebrow and mutter something about *"too many cooks and not enough plot."*

She rolled her eyes more than once.

But there was something about watching him write— something quietly intimate. His brow would furrow in concentration, lips occasionally moving with unsaid words, fingers stained with ink. He looked both older and younger when he worked—aged by grief, perhaps, but momentarily freed from it.

After nearly ninety minutes, he slid a sheet of paper across the table.

Harper took it, read it silently.

It was a monologue. A single page, written in the voice of a man addressing someone who had left him. The language was spare, poetic. Each line balanced on the edge of confession and restraint.

She read it twice.

Then looked up.

"Wow."

Elias didn't respond. Just stared at the window.

"It's... raw. Controlled, but emotional. There's a story here, underneath the words. A love story. A *real* one."

"It's not a story," he said. "It's a thought."

"Then let's build a story around it."

She began to outline possibilities. A character sketch. A fragmented plot. A sense of tension that could grow into something larger. She could see it—the flickers of a novel just starting to take shape, like sparks dancing at the edge of dry kindling.

"You're good at this," he said, interrupting her.

She blinked. "At outlining?"

"At seeing people."

Harper felt her throat tighten. She wasn't sure why that particular compliment landed like a pebble in her chest—soft, but sinking.

"I have to be," she said after a moment. "It's my job."

"But it's not what you want, is it?"

The question caught her off guard.

"What do you mean?"

"You talk about stories like you're outside of them. But I think you're supposed to be *inside* one. Writing it. Living it."

Harper shook her head. "I'm not a writer."

"No," Elias said. "But maybe you're afraid to be."

She tried to deflect. "That's rich, coming from you."

To her surprise, he laughed. A real laugh—low, rough, and brief.

"Touché."

The room quieted again, but something had shifted. The tension had softened. The sarcasm had gentled into something closer to curiosity.

They continued. They argued about voice. Perspective. Whether or not it was cheating to open a book with a flashback. Elias insisted it was lazy; Harper argued that, when done well, it was disarming.

By the time she looked at her phone, the sun had begun its descent over the sea, painting the horizon in watercolor shades of gold and mauve.

She blinked at the time. "I should go."

29

Elias nodded, leaning back in his chair. "Tomorrow?"

Harper stood, gathering her things. "Yeah. Tomorrow."

As she stepped outside, the air sharp with the first edge of autumn, she glanced back at the cottage.

Elias stood in the doorway, arms crossed, watching her leave.

Neither of them said anything.

But for the first time, Harper felt like a door had opened.

And this time, it hadn't slammed shut behind her.

***

Back at the Fog & Fern, Harper sat cross-legged on the small upholstered bench beneath her window, her notebook resting open in her lap. Outside, the sun was dipping below the horizon, casting long streaks of fire across the surface of the water. She wasn't ready for dinner. She wasn't even sure she was hungry. Her mind was still tangled in the quiet electricity of the afternoon.

She couldn't stop thinking about Elias's writing.

There was something in his prose—restrained, aching—that burrowed under her skin. He wrote like a man teetering on the edge of something enormous. A truth he didn't want to face. A past he hadn't forgiven. His words weren't just beautiful; they were *haunted*. Each sentence hummed with grief and longing, like he was writing from some narrow space between memory and regret.

But there was also control. Discipline. She recognized the signs—he hadn't stopped being a writer. He'd just stopped believing it mattered.

And maybe, she thought, *so have I.*

Harper closed her notebook and leaned back against the wall, staring at the ceiling. She let her thoughts drift, first toward Elias, then toward herself.

She hadn't always been this hardened. There had been a time—long before Quinn Literary, long before her daily life was an endless parade of rejection letters and trend forecasting—when stories had been magic. She'd grown up in a noisy, uneven household in Jersey with two younger brothers, a single mother who worked double shifts at the hospital, and stacks of library books always threatening to take over her room. Books had been her escape. Her secret language. The only space where she felt like herself.

By the time she was sixteen, she had a wall full of highlighted quotes and character names scrawled in the margins of her notebooks. In college, she'd worked in the campus bookstore and spent her evenings editing friends' short stories—not for money, just for the thrill of coaxing better words from raw ones.

She never wanted to write. Not really. But she *loved* helping others tell their stories.

At least, she used to.

Then came the agency. The long hours. The first promotion. The first big client—then the first one to leave. By the time she hit thirty, she was spending more time reading algorithms than manuscripts.

It had been a long time since she'd looked at words and felt something other than fatigue.

Until today.

She didn't want to admit how much it shook her.

***

At the cottage, Elias washed the ink from his fingers in the kitchen sink, scrubbing harder than necessary.

He hadn't meant to write as much as he had. At first, he thought he'd give her a single paragraph, let her use it as a bone to chew on and leave it at that. But something about the way Harper sat—sharp, focused, always watching, but not in a predatory way—had made it hard to hide.

She wasn't like the editors he'd dealt with before the fire.

She didn't circle him like prey or treat his words like golden eggs. She challenged him. She pushed. But she listened, too.

And damn it all, she was right.

He *had* been writing. In notebooks. On napkins. In margins of newspapers. Never anything he thought of as real. Never enough to form the bones of something new. But those entries weren't just reflections.

They were bleeding.

And when she'd read them aloud, something stirred that he thought he'd buried under layers of guilt and ash.

He stared out the window at the ocean, the sky now bleeding pink into blue.

It had been nearly ten years since the fire.

Ten years since Claire's laugh had echoed in these rooms. Since her humming filled the kitchen while she made tea. Since she'd stood behind him as he wrote, fingers grazing his shoulders, reminding him to breathe.

And in one night, all of it was gone.

People thought grief dulled with time.

But Elias knew better.

Grief didn't dull. It just learned to hide.

He turned from the window, unable to look at the waves anymore. That night was always in the waves—the way they crashed and receded, pulled things under.

He walked to the fireplace and stoked the logs, the dry crackle filling the silence. Then, almost without thinking, he returned to the table and opened the black journal Harper had read from.

Her fingers had touched these pages.

And somehow, that mattered.

***

The next morning, Harper walked to the inn's dining room to find Irene already setting out fresh scones, scrambled eggs, and a pot of tea that smelled like cinnamon and orange peel.

"You look different," the innkeeper said, her tone casual but curious.

Harper blinked. "Different how?"

"Lighter."

Harper let out a breath that was half a laugh. "I think I forgot what it feels like to want to read someone's words. Not just sell them."

"Then you're doing something right," Irene said, pouring tea into a china cup. "He's a quiet man, Elias. But quiet doesn't mean empty."

"No," Harper said softly. "It really doesn't."

They ate in comfortable silence. Outside, a breeze rustled the trees, sending a few early red leaves drifting past the window.

Harper excused herself, packed up her things, and headed out again. The cottage had begun to feel less like a stranger's home and more like a destination. Like the plot point after the inciting incident—the place where everything might shift.

As she drove, she thought about the story they were trying to write. The prompt had been vague. A man unable to tell the truth. But what if the real heart of the story wasn't what he *couldn't* say... but what he was afraid someone else might *hear*?

The stakes weren't always in the plot. Sometimes they lived in the character's chest.

She thought about Elias's line from the day before:

I only knew how to whisper pain. I think she heard me anyway.

It was more than a line. It was a map.
And she was starting to see the way forward.

***

When Harper arrived at the cottage that morning, Elias didn't greet her with words. He simply opened the door and stepped aside, allowing her in with a nod and a mug of fresh black coffee.

Progress, she thought, biting back a smirk.

The smell of toast and cedar hung in the air. The fireplace was lit again—even though it wasn't strictly cold—and music played softly from a record player in the living room: a Miles Davis album spinning with faint crackles between notes.

She followed him down the hall to the writing room, where sunlight streamed across the large oak table.

A fresh legal pad sat on the surface, next to his black journal and a pencil worn down to a nub. Harper set her bag down and slid into her now-regular seat.

"I was thinking about yesterday," she began, flipping open her notebook.

"That's usually dangerous," Elias replied, already scribbling something in the margin of his pad.

"I meant the story," she said. "The character we talked about—the one who can't tell the truth. I kept coming back to this idea: what if the lie he's telling isn't for protection? What if it's his way of honoring someone he lost? A way to preserve a memory that's already crumbling?"

Elias's pencil paused mid-scratch.

"You're not describing a liar," he said. "You're describing a man in mourning."

Harper's tone softened. "Exactly."

For a moment, neither spoke. The only sound was the quiet rasp of Elias's pencil and the occasional caw of gulls outside.

Then he said, "Let's give him a name."

"James," Harper said without hesitation.

Elias looked at her. "That was quick."

"It's always James. When I don't know who a man is yet, he's James."

Elias made a small noise—something between a grunt and a laugh. "And the woman?"

Harper blinked. "You think there's a woman?"

"There's always a woman," he said, voice low. "Even if she's gone."

Harper nodded slowly. "Then she's called Evelyn."

"James and Evelyn," Elias murmured, as if trying the names on like old coats.

He wrote something else down. Harper craned her neck to see, but he shielded the page with his forearm.

"Do I get to look?" she asked.

"When I've decided it's worth sharing."

"Always a critic."

"You hired me for it."

"I didn't hire you. You're freelance trauma."

That made him laugh. Really laugh. It surprised both of them.

It was short, but genuine—and Harper realized, in that moment, that she'd never seen Elias look younger. His face, usually drawn with shadows and angles, relaxed. The effect was startling. There was a version of him underneath the grief, buried deep but not unreachable.

She liked that version.

Too much.

They worked for over two hours, drafting character backstories, sketching out a rough arc that Harper cautiously labeled *Act I—Before the Truth*. Elias resisted all talk of outlines and plot points, so Harper offered structure without calling it that—posing open-ended questions, challenging his phrasing, pushing him to dig one layer deeper with each pass.

It became a rhythm.

He'd write a paragraph. She'd read it, question it, and ask for more.

And slowly, a narrative began to emerge.

James was a man who had loved once, and lost. Not in a tragic accident, not in a single explosive moment—but slowly, incrementally, until he woke up one day and realized the life he'd built no longer contained the person he remembered loving.

Evelyn, meanwhile, was more memory than woman—vibrant in fragments, missing in the present. And yet, somehow, she shaped every decision James made.

It wasn't a romance.

Not exactly.

But it was intimate.

And heartbreakingly human.

At some point, Harper stood and began to pace, too full of ideas to sit still. Elias watched her from behind his journal, one brow arched.

"You always move like that when your brain is on fire?" he asked.

She didn't stop. "I think better when I move. It's a hazard of city living. We pace to stay sane."

"You mean to avoid the quiet."

She stopped. Turned toward him.

"That too."

Elias closed the journal.

"What did you do before publishing?"

Harper blinked. "What?"

"You're good with people. Sharp. But you ask questions like a therapist and dig like a reporter. So what came before agenting?"

She hesitated, then returned to the table and sat across from him.

"I studied psychology for a year. Switched to English after I realized I didn't want to analyze people—I wanted to understand them on my own terms."

Elias nodded, eyes narrowing. "You still analyze. Just with different tools."

She leaned in. "What about you? What did you do before you were *Elias Stone, literary icon and recluse extraordinaire*?"

A faint smile tugged at the corner of his mouth. "I was a bartender."

Harper blinked. "You're kidding."

"Nope. Best training I ever had. You learn fast what people hide behind their drink orders."

"What's the saddest drink order?"

He didn't hesitate. "Gin and tonic. Ordered quietly."

She laughed, soft and genuine. "I've ordered that."

"I know."

They were quiet for a beat.

The sunlight shifted across the table. Outside, the breeze picked up again, blowing a paper across the surface. Elias caught it absently and pressed it back down.

"I didn't think I'd do this again," he said finally. "Sit at a table with someone who wasn't afraid to press the bruise."

Harper folded her hands. "I didn't come here to break you, Elias."

"I know," he said. "That's why it's working."

She didn't know what to say to that.

So she just nodded. And for a few heartbeats, they sat in the kind of silence that felt earned.

Then, trying to steady the energy, she asked, "So... what comes next for James?"

Elias considered the question.

"Maybe," he said slowly, "he meets someone who reminds him that he's still allowed to tell his story. That not all memories have to be sacred. Some can be shared."

Harper scribbled it down.

"Good," she said. "That's really good."

He looked at her, and in his gaze was something curious, unspoken. Like a question he wasn't ready to ask. Or maybe a thank-you he wasn't ready to say.

Either way, it lingered.

And neither of them looked away.

***

That afternoon, after several hours of steady work, Harper stepped outside to get some air. Elias had gone to refill their coffee, which she was beginning to suspect was more of a ritual than a necessity. She wandered to the edge of the bluff behind the cottage, where a rough stone bench faced the Atlantic.

The wind tugged at her coat, and the ocean crashed far below in a rhythmic, restless chant. The sun was bright now but low in the sky, casting long shadows over the cliffside.

She sat, letting the sea speak while her thoughts unraveled.

She'd shared very little of herself with Elias so far—strategically, professionally. She'd kept things in her domain: craft, business, story. It was safer that way. Distance gave her control.

But control was starting to feel like a kind of dishonesty.

He'd shared more with her already than she had with him. Not in confessions—he wasn't the type for sob stories—but in presence. In allowing her into his world, his process, even his quiet grief.

And if they were really going to write something honest together—

if that's what this was becoming—she owed him the same.

When she walked back inside, Elias was in the kitchen, pouring two mugs of dark roast. He handed one to her without a word, and she followed him back to the writing room.

Instead of sitting across from him, she took the seat beside him.

He didn't comment, but she saw the flicker of surprise in his eyes before he turned back to the table.

She opened her notebook, then closed it again.

"I want to tell you something," she said.

He glanced at her. "This sounds ominous."

"It's not." She folded her hands around the mug, fingers tense. "It's just... personal."

Elias set his mug down. Waited.

Harper drew in a breath. "There was someone. A few years ago. His name was Liam. We met at a publishing event—he was managing a tech startup that specialized in ebook distribution. Smart, charming, painfully patient with my schedule. We dated for nearly a year."

Elias said nothing. Just listened.

"I thought he was it. The real thing. We talked about moving in together. About traveling. About a future." She paused. "And then, one day, I walked into his apartment to surprise him. And I found him on a Zoom call... with another woman... who was clearly not just his business partner."

She gave a soft, bitter laugh.

"He told me later it had been going on for months. That I was too 'closed off.' That I was more focused on clients than connection. That he didn't feel 'chosen.'" She made air quotes around the word.

Elias frowned. "That's a hell of a word to throw around when you're cheating."

"Right?" she said. "But here's the thing—I believed him."

Elias looked at her, surprised. "You thought it was your fault?"

"I didn't *know* it wasn't." Her voice was calm, but underneath, the wound still pulsed. "I started wondering if I'd built my entire identity around being competent instead of... being vulnerable. If maybe he was right, and I just didn't know how to be loved in the way people needed me to be."

A long silence followed.

When she looked up, Elias was watching her. Not pitying— never that—but something quieter. Warmer.

"You know what I hear?" he said.

"What?"

"That you loved someone who didn't know how to see you. That's not your failure. That's his."

Harper blinked, taken aback by the gentleness in his voice.

"I'm not good at talking about this," she admitted.

"You just did."

She shook her head. "It's easier when it's for someone else. A client, a story. I know how to help *them* process it. But when it's my own... I shut down. I compartmentalize. And I think I've been doing that for so long, I forgot how much I've cut myself off."

Elias leaned back in his chair.

"That's why you read my pages like they mattered," he said.

"What do you mean?"

"Because you recognized the silence between the lines."

She swallowed. "Yeah. Maybe I did."

Another quiet stretched between them.

"I'm sorry," she said. "That I've kept you at arm's length."

Elias shook his head. "I don't mind the distance. What bothers me is when people pretend it's not there."

That hit harder than she expected.

He stood and walked to the window. The sun had slipped lower, the horizon melting into hues of copper and rose. The ocean glinted like a mirror—worn, beautiful, constant.

"You're not what I expected," he said, not turning around.

Harper tilted her head. "What did you expect?"

"A literary shark in designer heels. Someone who'd flash a contract and use charm like a crowbar." He paused. "But you came here with patience. With curiosity. And now I think you came with something else."

She stood, stepping closer to him. "What?"

"Loneliness."

The word cracked the air open between them.

Harper didn't deny it. Couldn't.

"Maybe I did."

Elias turned, and for the first time, she saw something in his expression that wasn't guardedness or irony or detachment.

It was understanding.

Recognition.

Not of her job. Not of her purpose.

Of *her*.

She looked at him, really looked—at the way his grief had shaped his quiet. At the way his posture still bent slightly toward someone who was no longer there. At the hands that once held more than ink and paper.

And she thought, *this is not a man who stopped writing.*

This is a man who's still in the middle of the story.

"I think we can help each other," she said.

"I think we already are," he replied.

***

By the time Harper and Elias returned to the writing table, the light in the room had shifted from golden to soft gray. Shadows stretched long across the floor, and the ocean outside had turned a deeper, inkier blue. The house creaked occasionally—settling, perhaps listening.

They sat side by side again. This time, closer.

Harper adjusted her notes, flipping back to their initial character work. "We've got names. We've got trauma. We've got setting. Time to get dangerous."

Elias raised an eyebrow. "You sound excited."

"I live for Act One. It's the cleanest part of the story. You still believe you're in control."

He smirked. "That's the delusion, isn't it?"

"Exactly. First chapters are little liars." She turned a page in her notebook and tapped her pen. "So—James. Where do we meet him?"

Elias didn't answer right away. Instead, he stared at the grain of the table, eyes distant.

Harper let the silence stretch. She'd learned that with him, pauses weren't obstacles. They were part of the process— breath between notes.

"He's at a hotel," Elias said finally. "Cheap. Coastal. The kind of place that still smells like cigarettes, even after they've scrubbed the wallpaper."

Harper nodded, already writing. "And?"

"It's raining. Hard. He's standing by the window, watching the road, waiting for someone who's not coming."

She paused mid-scribble. "How long has he been waiting?"

Elias's voice was low. "Years."

A chill rippled across her arms.

"Is he running from something?"

"More like trying to find a place where the memory doesn't follow him."

Harper met his eyes. "And he hasn't found it yet?"

"No." A pause. "Because it's not a place. It's a person. And she's already gone."

Harper nodded slowly. "That's a hell of a first scene."

Elias pushed his journal toward her. "Then let's write it."

They began to draft—trading lines, shaping sentences together in a rhythm that was half conversation, half dance. Harper would suggest a line of dialogue; Elias would pare it down, sharpen it. He'd build a scene in three lines; she'd push it into five, adding subtext and motion. Their styles were different—Harper wrote with clarity and structure, Elias with poetic weight—but together, something began to bloom.

They didn't speak as they worked, not much. But they moved in tandem. When Harper reached for a thesaurus, Elias slid it across the table before she asked. When Elias hesitated over a metaphor, Harper offered one that made his lips twitch in reluctant approval.

By the time the first draft of the scene was complete, they sat back in mutual stillness, like runners after a long sprint.

Harper looked down at the page.

> *The motel window rattled in its frame, the glass sweating with condensation. James didn't bother turning on the light. The rain did most of the talking anyway—tap tap tapping across the roof like fingers trying to wake a ghost. He didn't look at the empty bed. He hadn't touched it. Not since he'd checked in. There was no point. She wasn't coming. He'd known it the moment he booked the room.*

She let out a slow breath. "That's... good."

Elias didn't reply. He was watching her.

Not the page.

Her.

"You change when you write," he said.

Harper blinked. "Excuse me?"

"You get quiet. Still. Focused in this... unguarded way. It's like watching someone hold their breath without knowing they are."

She looked away, embarrassed. "I'm not used to doing this with someone else in the room."

"You mean writing?"

She nodded. "Writing. Thinking. Feeling things I don't have an immediate use for."

Elias considered that. "You're used to making meaning. Not sitting in the mess of it."

Harper met his gaze. "That's not a criticism?"

"It's an observation."

She smiled faintly. "Spoken like a man who *lives* in the mess."

"Someone has to."

They sat in silence again, the unspoken thing between them pressing closer now. A sense of proximity—intellectual, emotional, even physical. The kind of nearness that had nothing to do with distance and everything to do with the pause before you said something you couldn't take back.

Harper's voice was soft when she finally asked, "Why me, Elias?"

He looked puzzled.

"I mean it. You hadn't spoken to anyone about writing in years. Why open the door for *me*?"

Elias stared into the fire, thoughtful. "I read an article about you. A few years back. One of those trade magazine pieces— 'Ten Young Agents Reshaping the Literary World.'" He paused. "Most of it was fluff. Quotes about trends and platforms. But yours stood out."

She blinked. "What did I say?"

"You said something like: *'A good book doesn't save the reader. It saves the writer first.'*"

Harper's chest tightened.

"I remember that interview," she said. "I almost asked them to cut that line. Thought it made me sound... sentimental."

"It made you sound honest," Elias said. "And I wasn't ready for that honesty back then. But when Eleanor reached out, and said she'd send someone I could talk to, I remembered the article."

Harper looked down, swallowing past the emotion in her throat.

"I'm not that person anymore," she whispered.

Elias turned to her. "Then become her again."

A silence followed, thick with invitation. Harper felt like she was standing at the edge of something—something more than a collaboration. More than words.

A story neither of them had meant to begin.

She reached for her bag. "I should go before the road fogs over."

He nodded. "Come back tomorrow?"

Her lips curved into a tired, genuine smile. "Try and stop me."

As she walked out into the evening light, her pulse steady but loud in her ears, she realized something strange:

She didn't feel like she was chasing a story anymore.

She felt like she was living one.

Terms and Conditions

The next morning, Harper arrived at the cottage with bagels, a notebook full of ideas, and a strange flutter beneath her ribs she refused to name.

Not excitement.

Not quite anxiety.

A charge in the air. Something between forecast and foreshadowing.

Elias opened the door before she could knock. Again. He wore the same flannel from yesterday, sleeves pushed up to his elbows, hair tousled like he hadn't touched a comb. His feet were bare on the hardwood floor.

"You brought food," he said, eyeing the bag in her hand.

"Don't act so surprised. I'm generous before noon."

"Noted." He stepped aside and let her in. "We have a problem."

"That was fast."

Harper followed him into the kitchen, where the coffee was already brewing and an open notebook sat on the counter beside a plate of half-peeled oranges. Elias motioned to it like it was a loaded weapon.

"I was up most of the night," he said, voice low, controlled. "Thinking. Writing. Trying to figure out what exactly it is we're doing."

Harper raised an eyebrow. "That sounds dangerously like progress."

"I don't mean the story. I mean... this."

He turned to face her fully. There was a sharpness in his expression that hadn't been there the day before—not anger, exactly, but caution. Like a man remembering that fire burns if you stand too close.

"I need rules," he said.

Harper tilted her head. "Rules."

"Yes. Boundaries. Guardrails. Whatever you want to call them."

"For the collaboration?"

"For everything."

She set the bag of bagels on the table and crossed her arms. "Alright. Lay them out."

Elias leaned against the counter. "Rule one: Nothing we write is autobiographical. No memoir, no thinly veiled fiction based on real events. This is not therapy. It's a story."

Harper nodded slowly. "I can agree to that. Mostly."

"Mostly?"

"If something *true* makes the story better, we don't ignore it just because it's uncomfortable."

He hesitated, then nodded. "Fine. But we don't mine real pain for narrative convenience."

"Deal. Next?"

"Rule two: I don't do deadlines. No pressure. No artificial urgency. We write when there's something worth writing."

She arched a brow. "Elias, I'm not here to squeeze you for a manuscript on commission. I'm here because I believe there's something in you worth saying. I'll work on your timeline—but you have to keep showing up."

"I am showing up."

"Then we're good."

He looked slightly amused. "You're taking this well."

"I'm adaptable."

He folded his arms. "Rule three: No digging into my personal life. No questions about the fire. No questions about Claire. If something relevant comes up in the writing, I'll decide whether it stays."

Harper didn't answer right away. The name—*Claire*—hung between them like a matchbook held just over an open flame.

"I'm not here to hurt you," she said quietly.

"I know."

"But stories don't come from silence."

"They do if you listen hard enough."

Another silence settled over them. This one sharp-edged.

Finally, Harper said, "Then I have a few rules of my own."

Elias raised an eyebrow. "Oh?"

"Rule one: I'm not your therapist. If you want to write about ghosts, I'll help you shape them into a story. But I'm not here to fix anything."

"I didn't ask you to."

"Good." She stepped closer, her gaze steady. "Rule two: Don't talk down to me because I work in publishing. I know the industry has its vultures, but I'm not one of them. I've earned every inch of my place at the table, and I'm not here to chase your name—I'm here to build something real."

Elias's expression softened, just slightly.

"And rule three?"

Her voice dipped. "If we're going to work like this—if we're going to tell a story together—we don't get to pretend the tension isn't real."

He stilled.

"What tension?"

She gave him a slow, measured look.

"The kind that makes it hard to tell if we're arguing about character motivation or trying not to cross a line."

Elias's jaw flexed. He looked away for a second, then back at her. "And what happens if we *do* cross it?"

Harper didn't flinch. "We deal with it. Honestly."

He was quiet for a long moment.

Then, to her surprise, he reached into the drawer beside the sink and pulled out a pen. Clicked it. Handed it to her.

"I can live with those terms," he said.

She took the pen, clicked it shut, and tucked it behind her ear.

"Good," she said. "Now let's get to work."

***

They returned to the writing room. The light had shifted again—later morning now, the sun streaming brighter across the wooden floor. Elias sat on one end of the oak table, Harper on the other. Between them, the story waited.

They resumed where they left off, reading over the motel scene again.

Harper tapped her pencil against the page. "It needs grounding. James is lost, yes—but we need to feel the stakes sooner."

"Suggestions?"

"Give him an object. Something small. Personal. A photograph. A ring. A watch. A thing that ties him to her."

Elias nodded. "A key."

Harper looked up. "A key?"

"To a place that no longer exists."

A chill ran down her spine. "I like that."

They added the detail—James slipping the key out of his pocket, tracing its shape like a ritual. It opened nothing. And yet, he carried it still.

"Symbolism," Harper said, jotting a margin note. "Nice."

Elias leaned back. "You're starting to sound like a writer."

She smiled. "Don't curse me."

They kept going.

Scene by scene, idea by idea, they laid the framework. Not a full plot—not yet—but the skeleton of something with heart. With pain. With possibility.

At one point, Harper stood to stretch, walking over to the bookshelf. Her fingers trailed the spines of the novels—some dusty, others heavily dog-eared. She pulled down one of Elias's own books—*The Light Beneath*—and flipped to a passage she remembered.

He noticed. "That one's old."

"It holds up."

She read the passage aloud:

"Sometimes the places we go to be alone are just mirrors. And eventually, we have to decide if we like what we see."

Elias looked at her. "I hated that line when it went to print."

Harper turned to him. "Why?"

"Because it was true. And I wasn't ready to hear it."

She closed the book. "You think you are now?"

His answer was a long, slow breath.

"I'm trying."

She returned to the table and sat across from him. "That's all a good story needs."

***

The late morning sun was too tempting to ignore.

After a few hours of work inside, Harper stood, stretched, and looked toward the open window where the sea breeze teased the curtains. "We should take a break," she said, rubbing the back of her neck. "Some fresh air might shake something loose."

Elias, mid-sentence in a margin note, looked up. "You don't like to sit still, do you?"

"I do," she said. "Just not when I'm starting to think in circles."

He considered, then nodded. "Alright. But I'm not hiking."

"No hiking," she agreed. "Just... sitting in a different place."

They ended up on the bluff behind the cottage, on the old stone bench that faced the endless expanse of blue. The cliffs dropped steeply below, where waves rolled in and broke like thoughts never finished. Seagulls floated on invisible currents above them. The sky had cleared completely, and the ocean reflected it—bright, vast, deceptively calm.

Elias handed Harper a cup of coffee he'd poured into an old metal thermos. She took it without comment.

They sat in silence for a while, not because they didn't have anything to say—but because it was becoming easier, with each passing hour, to *be* silent around each other.

It felt strangely intimate.

Harper was the first to speak. "Can I ask you something?"

"You just did."

She shot him a side-eye glare. "Seriously."

Elias nodded, eyes still on the sea. "Go on."

"What's the thing that scares you most—when you write?"

He didn't hesitate. "Being understood."

That answer caught her off guard. "I expected you to say failure. Or cliché."

He smirked, but it faded quickly. "Failure is easy. You fail, you move on. You fail enough times, people stop expecting anything from you, and that's its own kind of freedom. But being understood?" He exhaled slowly. "That's a kind of nakedness you can't come back from."

Harper watched him, curious. "Why is that scary?"

"Because if they understand you, and they *still* leave... then it wasn't a misunderstanding. It was a rejection."

She was quiet for a long time.

Then she said, "That's not just a writer's fear. That's a human one."

Elias nodded once.

"What about you?" he asked. "What scares you most?"

She thought about it.

About the slush pile of manuscripts in her inbox. The ones she'd rejected, sometimes too quickly. About the clients she'd championed who'd ghosted her the minute another agent offered a bigger platform. About all the times she'd convinced herself she didn't care—until she realized she did, just too late to say so.

"Disappearing," she said finally.

Elias looked over.

"I'm terrified that one day, I'll wake up and realize I spent my whole life making other people visible... but never let anyone see *me*."

His gaze held hers for a long moment.

"You know," he said slowly, "for someone who doesn't write, you sure talk like a novelist."

"Don't start."

"I'm serious."

Harper sipped her coffee to avoid answering.

"I think that's why we're able to work like this," Elias continued. "You're not just editing me. You're reflecting something back."

Harper studied him. The light hit the side of his face, catching in the streaks of gray near his temples. He looked like a man suspended between past and present, like time had given up trying to place him in one or the other.

She wanted to ask more. About Claire. About the fire. About the years lost in silence. But she held back.

Not because of his rule.

Because of *respect*.

He'd told her what he could. The rest would come in time—if it came at all.

"You ever think about publishing again?" she asked instead. "For real?"

He gave a tired laugh. "Not until recently."

"Because of me?"

He didn't answer. Just looked back out at the ocean.

Which was, Harper realized, answer enough.

They sat for a while longer, letting the sea fill the space where their thoughts had paused. There was a rhythm to their silence now. Not avoidance, but cadence.

Finally, Elias stood. "Back to work?"

Harper nodded. "Yeah. Let's go find out what James does with that key."

***

Back inside, they resumed writing—this time focusing on the second scene. James was driving through a storm, the key in his coat pocket, headed toward a town that Evelyn used to love. But the place had changed. The storefronts were different. The café she adored was gone. The only thing left unchanged was the water. And even that seemed more bitter now.

As Harper dictated a few lines of dialogue, Elias watched her carefully.

"You talk like someone who's lived this," he said.

She didn't look up. "Everyone's lived this. It's called grief."

"But not everyone can describe it."

She finished the sentence she was writing, then met his eyes. "And you don't give yourself enough credit for the fact that you still *feel* it."

He blinked. "You think that's the point?"

"No." She smiled faintly. "I think it's the starting line."

They worked another hour, and by the time Harper stood to leave, the second scene was done. It wasn't perfect, but it was raw, real, and strangely cohesive—two voices shaping one story without stepping over each other.

She gathered her things.

Elias walked her to the door, leaning against the frame as she stepped onto the porch.

"Same time tomorrow?" she asked.

He nodded. "Unless you get tired of me."

She gave him a look. "I'm not that lucky."

He smiled. The real kind. The slow, reluctant kind that lived in the corners of his mouth and made him look ten years younger.

Harper turned and walked to her car, the gravel crunching beneath her boots.

As she pulled out of the driveway and drove away from the sea, her fingers tapped the steering wheel absently, and her mind kept circling one line he'd said.

Being understood is a kind of nakedness you can't come back from.

She thought maybe that was what they were building.

Not just a novel.

But understanding.

And it scared her just enough to know she'd show up tomorrow without question.

***

Harper sat on the floor of her inn room, legs stretched out beneath the window, her notebook open across her lap. The sea breeze wafted through a cracked windowpane, cool and laced with salt. A mug of tea sat untouched beside her.

She had been staring at the same blank page for nearly fifteen minutes.

The words wouldn't come.

Not the way they usually did, neat and efficient, dressed in bullet points or query-ready phrases. No polished sales copy, no editorial feedback. Just… emotion. Vague, unfiltered, messy emotion. And she hated it.

She flipped to a new page and forced herself to write a single word in the center:

"Why?"

Why was she still here?

Why was she waking up early to drive to a man who hadn't written in a decade?

Why did it feel like something inside her was stretching, cracking—both painful and inevitable?

She tapped the pen to the page. Then wrote, without editing:

"It's not just about the book.

It's about the quiet I feel when I'm around him.

The quiet that doesn't demand I perform.

The quiet that feels like breath, not suffocation."

She stared at the words.

Then slammed the notebook shut.

This was a problem. A *very* real problem.

She had come to Elias's cottage to help him write again—not to become part of the story. Not to feel her own silence reflected back at her with such terrifying accuracy. Not to start asking questions she'd spent years outrunning.

Things like:

What if connection wasn't weakness?
What if her ambition wasn't protecting her, but isolating her?
What if she was more afraid of being loved than she was of being alone?

She stood up, moved to the mirror above the small writing desk, and stared at her reflection. Her hair was windswept, her eyeliner slightly smudged from hours of focus and salt air. She looked... undone.

But not broken.

Not yet.

She pressed a hand to her chest, grounding herself with the smallest touch, then whispered to the reflection, "You're here for the book. Stay on task."

But the mirror offered no promises.

***

Back at the cottage, Elias sat at the table alone, his chair pulled closer to the window than usual. He held a different notebook tonight—not the one Harper had seen. This one was smaller, bound in soft leather, with frayed edges and pages that had yellowed from years of air and ink.

Claire had given it to him.

For ideas, she'd said, when they'd still believed there would always be more stories. When writing was still just one of many things that tethered him to the world.

Elias hadn't written in this notebook in almost ten years.

But tonight, something in him felt unmoored. Harper's questions still lingered in the air. The look in her eyes when she said *"I'm terrified of disappearing."* The way she walked away like she already knew she'd be back.

He didn't know what this thing was between them—this collaboration, this closeness—but it was no longer just about plot structure and dialogue.

It was about the ache underneath it.

He uncapped his pen, and began to write:

> "Sometimes I hear her in the walls—
> not as a sound,
> but as a silence
> I used to mistake for peace.
> Now I know better.
> Peace doesn't hum like that.
> It doesn't carry guilt in its rhythm.
> I want to write again, but the words taste like her name.
> I'm afraid that telling a story
> will mean letting go of the one I've kept in my chest all these years—

the one where I keep her alive
by refusing to move forward."

He paused.
Then added:

"But Harper writes like someone who is still choosing
to move.
And maybe that's the only kind of person
who can remind the dead
that they're not the ones still breathing."

He closed the notebook before the ink dried, pressing the pages together like a secret.

He would not show her this.

Not yet.

Maybe not ever.

But writing it had shifted something in his chest. Not a release—more like the warning rumble before a fault line breaks.

He stood, walked to the fireplace, and stoked the flame. The wood snapped loudly in the silence, but the sound didn't startle him.

He was getting used to the quiet again.

Not the kind that haunted.

The kind that made room for someone else.

***

The next morning, Harper woke before her alarm.

She dressed slowly, choosing jeans and a navy sweater, pulling her hair into a loose braid she usually reserved for weekends or writing retreats she never took.

At breakfast, Irene raised a knowing brow as Harper poured coffee into her mug.

"You're glowing," the innkeeper said casually, like commenting on the weather.

Harper froze. "Excuse me?"

"You have that post-storm brightness. Like someone cracked open the clouds and let some truth in."

Harper laughed tightly. "That's poetic. Are you moonlighting as a novelist?"

Irene just smiled. "I'm old. I've seen what this looks like."

"What what looks like?"

"Two people trying very hard not to fall into something they're already knee-deep in."

Harper nearly choked on her coffee.

"I'm working," she said firmly. "That's all."

"Of course you are," Irene replied. "And I'm just a woman who makes muffins."

They both knew it wasn't that simple.

***

Harper arrived at the cottage to find Elias already seated at the writing table, a cup of tea beside him instead of coffee.

He didn't greet her with a quip. Just nodded toward her usual seat.

Harper sat.

"I had a thought," he said, sliding a fresh sheet of paper her way.

She read it quickly. It was a sketch—just a few lines of prose about Evelyn, James's lost love. Elias had imagined her as someone who saw through James's quiet, who asked questions he didn't know how to answer, who held his pain like it was worth something.

Harper recognized herself in every line.

She looked up.

"You're writing her like she's real," she said softly.

Elias's eyes didn't flinch. "She is."

Harper hesitated. "And James?"

He paused. "Becoming real."

That was all he said.

But it was enough.

***

The rain came in the late afternoon, sudden and loud, hammering against the windows of the cottage like an accusation. Thunder rumbled distantly, a low, constant growl that rattled through the floorboards. The sky outside was heavy and gray, as if the clouds themselves were grieving something unspeakable.

Inside, Harper and Elias sat at opposite ends of the oak table, the air between them no longer charged with curiosity—but tension.

Creative sessions, like any partnership, could shift suddenly. One minute they were aligned, building a scene with effortless harmony. The next, they were colliding.

And today, they were colliding.

"No," Elias said flatly, tossing his pencil down. "It's not working. It's too clean."

Harper frowned. "What do you mean, 'clean'? The dialogue's raw. It's stripped down. It's exactly how someone like James would speak—direct, defensive."

"It's predictable," Elias countered. "It reads like a therapy session with punctuation."

Harper bristled. "So rewrite it."

Elias leaned back, folding his arms across his chest. "That's not the problem. The problem is that it's emotionally convenient. There's no friction."

She snapped her notebook closed. "You asked for honesty. That's what this scene is. James isn't being clever, he's being vulnerable."

"And I'm saying it doesn't ring true."

"So say that instead of bulldozing the whole thing."

They stared at each other, the rain hammering harder against the cottage windows, making everything feel sharper. Wilder.

Harper stood and walked to the window, arms crossed, trying to cool the heat rising in her chest.

"You know what this really is?" she said, still facing the glass. "You're not worried the scene is bad. You're worried it's getting too close to the truth."

She turned to see Elias still seated, but his jaw was tight. His knuckles white around the pencil he'd picked back up.

"You want to tell James's story," she continued, "but only as long as it doesn't make *you* feel exposed. You keep calling it fiction, but the minute it scratches something real, you pull back."

"That's not true," he said quietly.

"Yes, it is."

Elias stood slowly. "You don't get to say that. You don't know what I'm pulling back from."

"Then tell me."

The room crackled. Not with thunder—but with something more dangerous: invitation.

Elias stepped forward. Just enough to narrow the space between them.

"You want the truth?" he said, voice low, tight. "Fine. Every time we write a scene about James losing Evelyn, I have to relive what it was like to stand in the street with nothing but smoke in my lungs and her name on my tongue."

Harper's heart thudded in her chest.

"I don't write slowly because I'm lazy," Elias continued. "I write slowly because every sentence drags the fire back. Because if I get it right—if I say the thing I've been trying not to say—I'm terrified I'll lose what little of her I've got left."

Harper opened her mouth, but he kept going.

"And yes, I pulled back. I always pull back. Because grief is easier to hold in your fists than in your mouth. But don't stand there and pretend you haven't done the same."

The air between them was charged, hot, unbearable.

Then Harper stepped forward, meeting his intensity with her own.

"You're right," she said, voice steady. "I have pulled back. From everyone. From *everything*. Because the last time I let someone in, he left, and told me it was because I couldn't love him right."

Elias blinked.

"And maybe I couldn't," Harper said, softer now. "Because I was too busy loving the idea of a future that didn't require me to be vulnerable. Too busy proving I was capable, untouchable, independent. But I *wasn't*. And when he left, I didn't fight. I just packed it up. Buried it."

Silence.

Only the rain answered.

Elias stepped back.

Ran a hand through his hair.

"I'm not good at this," he said, voice rough.

Harper let out a shaky breath. "Neither am I."

He sank into his chair, and for a moment, he looked exhausted. Not just physically—but soul-deep.

Harper sat too.

They didn't speak for a long while. The thunder rolled again in the distance, softer this time. The worst of the storm was passing.

Finally, Elias spoke.

"I don't want to ruin this."

Harper looked at him. "This?"

He met her eyes. "Whatever this is."

She nodded slowly. "Then don't."

They sat in the stillness, the space between them less like a chasm now and more like a page—blank, waiting, full of possibility.

After a few minutes, Elias reached for the discarded pencil and slid the scene back toward them.

"You were right," he said quietly. "James would say it. He just wouldn't say it like that."

Harper pulled the notebook back toward her. "Then let's try again."

Together, they began rewriting the scene—this time slower, more carefully. Every line sharpened. Every silence respected. The words came not from their heads, but from the places they hadn't dared look the day before.

And when they finished, Elias said something Harper would remember long after the book was done.

"This isn't just fiction anymore," he said.

She didn't disagree.

Because she knew exactly what he meant.

***

The rain had stopped.

By late evening, the clouds began to thin, leaving behind a bruised sky that turned purple at the edges. The windows glistened with remnants of the storm. The fire crackled low in the hearth, casting flickering shadows against the cottage walls.

Harper sat curled into the armchair near the fire, a blanket over her legs, tea cooling in her mug. She was reading over their revised scene for the third time—not because she doubted it, but because something in it still pulled at her. The voice was clearer now. The pain sharper. James had come alive, not as a proxy or placeholder, but as a man who felt real in the space between their sentences.

Elias had gone into the kitchen to find more tea. He'd been quieter since the fight—softened, maybe, or just tired. Something about the argument had changed the energy between them, but not in a way that felt like damage.

It felt like progress.

The door to the writing room was slightly ajar, and as Harper stood to stretch her legs, she wandered toward it, notebook still in hand.

Inside, the long oak table was still cluttered with notes, scraps, drafts, and empty tea mugs. The rain had fogged the windows, and the room glowed dimly in the evening light.

She reached for a folder that had been left slightly open at the far end of the table—one she hadn't noticed before. It wasn't labeled. Just a stack of loose, handwritten pages bound by a fraying leather cord.

Harper hesitated.

Then, carefully, she opened it.

The first page was written in Elias's distinct hand. The date in the corner—two weeks ago—jumped out at her. This wasn't old. This was recent.

She scanned the first few lines.

Sometimes I hear her in the walls—
not as a sound,
but as a silence
I used to mistake for peace...

69

Harper's chest tightened.

This wasn't fiction. These were his private thoughts—his raw, unfiltered grief etched onto the page like confessionals. She shouldn't be reading this.
She knew it.
But she couldn't look away.

> *I want to write again, but the words taste like her name.*
> *I'm afraid that telling a story*
> *will mean letting go of the one I've kept in my chest all these years—*
> *the one where I keep her alive*
> *by refusing to move forward.*

It was the most vulnerable version of Elias she'd ever seen.
And suddenly, Harper understood.
All of it.

The hesitation. The fear. The deep restraint in his writing. This wasn't just about a lost wife or a shelved manuscript. It was about identity. Guilt. The paralysis of loving someone so much, you didn't know who you were without the ache.

She gently closed the folder and replaced it exactly as she'd found it.

The door creaked softly as she stepped back into the living room, just as Elias returned with two fresh mugs of tea.

"You disappeared," he said, handing her one.

"Stretching my legs." She took the mug, wrapped both hands around it, and returned to her armchair.

He settled across from her, watching her over the rim of his cup. "You okay?"

Harper hesitated. "You ever write something you didn't want anyone to read, but also kind of hoped they would?"

Elias's gaze sharpened. "Did you find something?"

She looked at him over the rim of her mug. "Just a thought."

He didn't press, but the pause between them grew heavier, more aware.

"I've written a lot of things I didn't want anyone to see," he said eventually. "Not because I was hiding—but because I wasn't ready to explain."

Harper nodded slowly. "Maybe some things aren't meant to be explained."

He looked down at his tea. "Or maybe they just need the right reader."

The words hovered.

Then, with a quiet shift in energy, Harper asked, "Do you miss it?"

"Writing?"

She nodded.

Elias leaned back, eyes fixed on the fire. "I miss the moments when I forgot I was the one doing it. When it felt like the story was pulling me somewhere I didn't know I needed to go."

"Sounds a lot like faith."

"Maybe it was."

Harper took a breath. "And now?"

He looked at her, then—to her surprise—reached over to the stack of drafts on the table beside them. He pulled one page free and handed it to her.

"Now," he said, "it feels like a return."

She read the page. It wasn't a scene. Not really. More like a memory reimagined.

He remembered the sound of her laugh in an empty room.
It had always echoed. Not loudly—just enough to remind him
that silence was never truly still.

Harper looked up, blinking against the weight of it.

"It's beautiful," she said softly.

"It's unfinished."

She handed it back. "So keep writing."

Their fingers brushed for a moment as he took the page.

Neither pulled away.

Neither spoke.

They didn't have to.

The room was still. The rain had stopped. Outside, the wind had died down, and the night sky was starting to clear. Stars began to poke through the black velvet above, faint but unwavering.

Harper stood, smoothing her sweater. "I should go."

Elias didn't stand. But he watched her like he was memorizing the shape of her as she moved.

She walked to the door, then paused with her hand on the knob.

When she turned back, her eyes met his.

"I'm not here to save you, Elias."

His expression softened. "I know."

"I'm just here to write with you."

A small, grateful smile tugged at the corner of his mouth. "That's the first time I've felt like maybe I can."

She nodded, then stepped outside into the cool, damp night.

As she walked toward her car, her heart beat harder than it should have.

Because she knew the truth.

This wasn't just about writing anymore.

Not for either of them.

***

Sentences & Silence

The following morning, Harper arrived at the cottage earlier than usual.

The sun had only just begun rising above the water, painting the ocean in pale golds and slate blues. Mist curled over the cliffs in lazy swirls, and for the first time in days, the world felt still.

She knocked out of habit but didn't wait for an answer.

Elias had told her the night before: *"Just come in. I trust you."*

It had been a quiet statement, said over shared tea and the scent of woodsmoke, but it had struck her harder than it should have. Because it hadn't been said casually.

And it hadn't been said often—by either of them.

Inside, the fire was already lit. The table had been cleared, a clean sheet of paper centered neatly in front of Elias's chair. A mug of coffee steamed beside it—his, not hers.

She found him in the kitchen, barefoot and half-awake, slicing an apple with slow precision.

"You're early," he said without looking up.

"You're making breakfast," she countered. "This is new."

He shrugged. "I ran out of excuses not to."

Harper leaned against the doorframe, arms folded. "Anything on your mind?"

Elias glanced at her. "Other than the woman who keeps showing up at my house to dig through my soul one sentence at a time?"

She smiled. "She sounds exhausting."

"She is."

But there was warmth in his voice, and something that hovered between teasing and gratitude.

They ate at the table—apples, toast, strong coffee—and reviewed the scenes they'd drafted over the past week. The novel was slowly forming, still skeletal but unmistakably alive. They had a title in their notes (*The Quiet Between Us*) and a tentative structure that hinged not on big twists, but on moments—small, quiet devastations.

James, their protagonist, had become something more than a man with a key in his pocket. He had depth now. Regret. Anger. Humor. He was still grieving, but the grief was no longer static.

Harper had begun referring to him as *ours*.

As in, "I think our James would hesitate here," or "Our James wouldn't say that line, not yet."

It was the kind of collaboration she hadn't had since her college lit mag days—when stories were still labors of love, not commercial blueprints.

They wrote for most of the morning, pausing only to refill their mugs or stretch stiff limbs. By noon, the page before them held a new scene: a conversation between James and a woman named Elise—Evelyn's sister, who had always seen the fractures in James's relationship, even when Evelyn had refused to.

Elise was honest. Blunt. Almost cruel in her clarity.

She was Harper's creation.

Elias didn't love her.

"She's too clean," he said, frowning.

"She's not clean," Harper said. "She's just not grieving."

"Exactly. That makes her dangerous."

Harper cocked her head. "Why? Because she isn't frozen in place?"

"Because she isn't *hesitating*."

Harper paused, then asked, carefully, "Is hesitation weakness to you?"

"No," Elias said softly. "It's humanity."

They rewrote Elise's dialogue. Softened the edges. Gave her a line that made Harper catch her breath:

> *"We don't stop loving people when they leave. But we can stop building altars where we should be building bridges."*

Harper read it aloud.

Elias looked away.

And just like that, the air changed again.

***

Later that day, Harper found herself alone in the writing room while Elias stepped out to feed the chickens. She was looking for an old draft when she noticed the narrow drawer in the table. One she hadn't opened before.

She hesitated.

Curiosity wasn't new to her—she made a career out of asking questions people didn't want to answer.

But this felt different.

Still, her fingers moved before her conscience could stop them.

Inside the drawer was a stack of papers yellowed at the corners. They weren't labeled, and there were no dates—but the handwriting was unmistakable. Elias's. Neat. Precise. Scrawled in blue-black ink.

The pages weren't the same style as the recent scenes they'd written together. These were denser. More chaotic. And as she flipped through the first few, her stomach clenched.

It was a novel.

Not the one they were writing now.

A different story. Older. Rawer.

The pages told of a fire. A woman lost. A man unraveling in the absence of a love so large it had swallowed him whole. The prose was lyrical, devastating, dangerously personal.

Harper realized, halfway through a particularly gutting paragraph, that this was *the* manuscript—the one Elias had abandoned the night Claire died. The book he never finished. The one he told no one had survived.

But here it was.

Unedited. Unpublished.

Breathing.

She closed the folder, hands shaking slightly.

When Elias returned, she was sitting by the window, staring out at the waves.

He paused, reading her posture like a line of text.

"What is it?" he asked.

"Nothing," she said too quickly.

He didn't press.

But Harper knew something had shifted inside her—something permanent.

She'd seen the version of Elias that still wrote in blood.

And she couldn't unread it.

***

Harper didn't sleep well that night.

She tossed under the quilt at the Fog & Fern, her mind cycling endlessly through Elias's hidden manuscript. Images from the pages blurred into dreams: a house engulfed in flames, a man screaming a name into smoke, a sentence that repeated like a broken metronome—*"She said she'd come back."*

She woke before dawn, tangled in the sheets, heart pounding.

It wasn't just the content of what she'd read.

It was the weight of what it meant.

Elias hadn't just abandoned that book—he'd buried it. Lied about it. Or, at the very least, hidden it so deeply even he refused to acknowledge it existed. And now Harper, who had promised not to dig, had unearthed it.

And worse?

She didn't regret it.

Not entirely.

That was the part that kept her pacing the small room, chewing her thumbnail and watching the light shift across the walls. Because some small, brutal part of her had needed to know. To *see* what he'd written when the grief was freshest. When his words weren't guarded or refined, but feral.

That manuscript had been raw, yes—but also alive. Messy. Lyrical. It was Elias's voice in its most honest form.

And it changed everything.

Not just how she saw him.

But how she saw the story they were writing now.

Because *this* Elias—the one sitting across from her every day, carefully crafting James's grief into something structured—was holding back.

And now that she knew what he was capable of, she couldn't *not* want more.

*****

When she arrived at the cottage that morning, she wore her best version of neutral: jeans, a loose cream sweater, and her "business casual" expression—pleasant, professional, unreadable.

Elias was already at the table, typing something into his old laptop. He glanced up when she walked in.

"Coffee's still hot," he said, gesturing to the French press on the counter.

"Thanks."

She poured herself a mug and took her seat across from him. Her notebook felt heavier in her hands today.

They worked in silence for nearly an hour, drafting the next scene between James and Elise. The words came, but slower. Less fluid. Elias wrote with more precision than usual, but also more restraint. Every sentence felt like it had passed through three filters before making it onto the page.

Harper noticed.

He did too.

"You're quiet today," he said after their third revision.

"So are you."

He leaned back in his chair. "I thought we were past pretending."

She kept her tone light. "I'm just thinking."

"About what?"

"James," she lied.

Elias watched her for a long beat.

Then, slowly, he closed his laptop and folded his hands on the table.

"Is something wrong?"

Harper hesitated. The truth burned in the back of her throat.

Say it, a voice in her head urged. Tell him you found the manuscript. That you read it. That you *felt* it.

But another voice—calmer, colder—warned: *If you break the silence, you might break the trust.*

So instead, she said, "I think we're holding back."

Elias's brow furrowed. "We?"

Harper nodded. "James is evolving, sure. But there's still something... missing."

"Missing how?"

She struggled to find the right words—truth adjacent, but not quite confession. "There's a tension in the story that we keep circling, but we're not letting it breathe. It's like we're afraid to let him fall apart."

Elias's eyes darkened slightly. "Maybe he doesn't need to fall apart."

"Or maybe he already has," she countered. "And we're just not letting the reader *see* it."

He stood, abruptly, and walked to the window. His shoulders were tense, and when he spoke again, his voice had cooled.

"Not every story needs to bleed all over the page."

"No," Harper agreed. "But every good one has a pulse. And lately, I can't feel ours."

He turned then, slowly. "Is this about the book?"

She blinked. "What else would it be about?"

Elias didn't answer.

Which, of course, *was* an answer.

They stared at each other in the silence, something tight and fragile between them. Not anger. Not yet. But the first echo of it. The suggestion that truth had become too crowded in the room.

Harper finally looked away. "Maybe we should take a break."

"From the book?" he asked, too quickly.

"Just for the day."

He hesitated, then nodded.

Harper gathered her things carefully, deliberately. When she passed by the writing room door on her way out, her hand brushed the edge of the drawer—the one with the manuscript still hidden inside.

She didn't open it again.

But she didn't forget it, either.

***

That evening, Elias sat alone in the cottage, the fire unlit for once, the shadows stretching long across the walls. He held the leather-bound draft in his lap, flipping pages with a kind of reverence that bordered on mourning.

He had known the moment Harper entered the room that morning that something had shifted.

She was too quiet. Too poised. Her silences, usually pregnant with thought, had turned evasive. Calculated.

And now he knew why.

She had found it.

His unfinished book.

The one he'd sworn he'd never show to anyone.

The one that had nearly burned him alive even after the fire had ended.

He thought about confronting her.

But what could he say?

Did you like it?

Did it hurt you the way it hurt me?

Did you read it and see Claire?

Did you read it and see yourself?

Instead, he returned it to the drawer.

Not out of shame.

But because he finally understood something:

Harper hadn't violated his trust.

She'd made him see that it still existed.

And maybe…maybe silence wasn't the safest thing he owned after all.

***

The Fog & Fern Inn smelled like rosemary and lemon butter.

Harper sat across from Irene at the long farmhouse table, nursing a glass of wine and pushing roasted carrots around her plate. The dining room was warm and homey, candles flickering in glass jars along the windowsill, the sound of rain still faintly echoing from the roof above.

It had been Irene's idea—*"You need food, not caffeine. And company, not characters."*

Harper had resisted at first, still tangled in the guilt of what she'd read at Elias's cottage, but eventually relented. Something about Irene made it impossible to keep your defenses up for too long. She was one of those women who saw through things. Not with judgment—but with clarity.

Now, Harper stared at her half-empty plate and tried to act normal.

Irene took a sip of her tea. "You're fidgeting."

Harper paused, her fork mid-air. "Am I?"

"Like someone trying to solve a math problem with her heart."

Harper gave a breathy laugh. "I'm not even sure what that means."

"You will."

They sat in silence for a beat. Then Irene leaned in, voice gentle.

"So. Are you going to tell me what happened?"

Harper hesitated, wineglass resting in both hands. "We hit a wall with the manuscript."

"'We,' huh?"

Harper rolled her eyes. "Yes. *We*. It's a collaborative project."

"You sure that's all it is?"

"I came here for the story."

"And you found a man instead."

Harper flushed. "That's not what I—"

"It's not an accusation, sweetheart. It's an observation."

Harper fell quiet again, staring at the way her wine reflected the soft glow of candlelight. Finally, she said, "He's... different."

Irene nodded knowingly.

"He's guarded. Quiet. But when he writes, it's like he opens a door in the middle of a hurricane and lets you stand there in the wind."

"That's a hell of a thing to say about someone you're not falling for."

Harper laughed—but it caught on something inside her. "I'm not falling."

Irene raised an eyebrow.

"I mean... not intentionally."

"That's usually how it works."

Harper rubbed her forehead, suddenly tired. "There's too much history there. Too much silence."

"Silence doesn't mean absence," Irene said. "It just means something's waiting to be heard."

Harper didn't reply.

But her fingers tapped the side of her glass. Quiet. Rhythmic. Like a code she didn't know how to break.

84

Meanwhile, back at the cottage, Elias stood in front of the fireplace, staring at a blank sheet of paper.

The storm outside had stilled, the clouds pulling back into the sky like smoke receding after a long burn. The cottage was quiet except for the occasional creak of old wood and the slow ticking of the clock above the mantel.

He sat down with the paper in his lap, a pen in his hand, and no idea what he was about to say.

But something Harper had said kept looping in his head:

"Every good story has a pulse."

He hadn't thought of his writing as living in a long time.

But maybe she was right.

He uncapped the pen and started to write—slowly, carefully—not about Claire, or the fire, or guilt.

But about now.

> *There is a kind of quiet that doesn't echo—it listens.*
> *The kind that exists not in the absence of pain,*
> *but in the presence of someone willing to sit with it.*
> *She doesn't ask for the whole story.*
> *She just asks if you're still telling it.*
> *And maybe that's the miracle.*
> *Not that she's reading —*
> *but that you're finally ready to be read.*

Elias stared at the words.

They weren't crafted.

They weren't for publication.

They were a truth he hadn't spoken aloud—not even to himself.

And they weren't about Claire.

They were about Harper.

He stood slowly, folded the paper, and slid it into a fresh notebook. One he hadn't used before. One not marked by grief, but by the unknown.

He didn't know if he'd show her.

Not yet.

But for the first time in ten years, he was writing toward something—not away from it.

***

Back at the inn, Harper returned to her room after dinner, Irene's words still clinging to her like sea mist.

"Silence doesn't mean absence. It just means something's waiting to be heard."

She opened her notebook and flipped past the pages filled with client notes and chapter outlines. Past the quotes she'd scribbled from Elias. Past the first scene of their novel.

She stopped on a blank page.

Then, in slow, looping script, she wrote:

> *Some silences are built like walls.*
> *But others—others are doorways.*
> *And it's terrifying to walk through one*
> *when you don't know what's waiting on the other side.*

She stared at the line.
Then added:

> *But if he's waiting there too...*
> *Maybe I won't need to say a word at all.*

***

The next morning, Harper arrived at the cottage early again. This time, she didn't hesitate when she opened the door.

Elias was already there, seated at the table with a cup of tea and a folded page in front of him. He looked up as she entered, and something passed between them—an acknowledgment without words. Neither of them smiled, but both softened.

"I have something for you," he said, tapping the paper.

Harper set her things down. "What is it?"

He pushed the page across the table without speaking.

She unfolded it carefully.

At first, she thought it was a poem. The line breaks. The shape of it on the page. But the more she read, the more she realized—it was a confession disguised as prose.

> *There is a kind of quiet that doesn't echo—it listens.*
> *The kind that exists not in the absence of pain,*
> *but in the presence of someone willing to sit with it...*

Her eyes skimmed the rest, heart racing faster with each line. It wasn't fiction. It wasn't James. It wasn't even Claire.

It was about *her.*

She looked up. "You wrote this last night."

He nodded. "After you left."

"It's… beautiful."

"It's unfinished," he said, echoing the phrase he'd used before. But this time, he wasn't hiding behind it.

Harper folded the page gently and set it on top of her notebook. "This doesn't belong in the drawer."

"I know."

They stared at each other for a long moment. The table between them no longer felt like a workspace. It felt like a border—one neither of them was quite ready to cross, but both were now facing with open eyes.

"So," she said quietly, "what do we do with that?"

Elias hesitated. Then shrugged, like he didn't trust words not to betray him. "We keep writing."

Harper nodded. "Alright."

***

They worked for most of the morning. This time, the words came easier. James was no longer frozen in grief. He was beginning to move, tentatively, awkwardly—like someone learning to breathe again. Their latest scene took place in a lighthouse, where James scattered the ashes of a letter he never sent.

It was Elias's idea.

"Burning the letter is more powerful than sending it," he said. "It's an ending disguised as an offering."

Harper nodded. "Or maybe a beginning disguised as an ending."

Either way, it worked.

The lighthouse scene was layered with symbolism—another bridge between memory and motion. When they finished, Harper leaned back in her chair and exhaled.

"This might be the best chapter yet."

Elias didn't respond immediately. He seemed to be watching her, not the page.

"What?"

He shook his head. "Just thinking."

She raised an eyebrow. "Dangerous habit."

Elias smiled faintly but said nothing more.

The silence between them, once strained, now felt like the pause between heartbeats.

***

The moment shattered when Harper's phone buzzed.

She glanced at the screen. Celia Warren—her boss at the agency.

Harper frowned. "I should take this. I'll step outside."

Elias nodded, eyes dropping to his notes.

Harper slipped out the front door and into the crisp morning light. She answered on the third ring.

"Celia, hey."

"Well, look who finally remembered she has a job."

Harper winced. "I've been sending updates."

"Updates are not progress, Harper. We signed Elias Blackstone to write a book, not to hide in the wilderness while you braid each other's emotional traumas into slow-burn scenes."

Harper's stomach knotted. "It's coming together. We've written over fifty pages. It's real. It's good."

"And when will I get a draft?"

"I don't want to rush him."

"You're not *his therapist,* Harper. You're his literary partner. Which means you have to manage expectations—even when the author is brooding and brilliant."

Harper swallowed hard.

Celia continued, her voice dropping. "The board's getting nervous. A reclusive author. No finished manuscript. No media updates. We've got a lot of investment riding on this comeback story—and if we don't deliver something tangible soon, we may lose our advance window."

"So you're threatening to pull out?"

"I'm saying," Celia said coldly, "you need to get him on record. An interview, a press statement, even a Q&A for the trades. Something. Or this deal goes on hold."

Harper pressed a hand to her forehead. "That will destroy his trust in me."

"Then maybe you should've considered that before going off-script."

"Celia—"

"Deadline. Three days. Either give me something I can use, or start packing your office."

The line went dead.

Harper stood in the wind for a long moment, phone still clutched in her hand.

The sea below was dark and restless. The same as her thoughts.

***

Back inside, Elias looked up as she reentered.

"You okay?" he asked.

Harper forced a smile. "Fine."

But Elias saw through it.

"Work trouble?"

She shrugged. "Just the usual. Expectations. Pressure."

He watched her carefully. "You want to talk about it?"

She shook her head. "Not right now."

He nodded, but she could see the concern lingering in his eyes.

They returned to the manuscript, but something had shifted. Harper's rhythm was off, her energy clipped. She kept glancing at her phone. Her handwriting was sharper, her revisions faster.

Elias didn't ask again.

But she could feel the questions radiating from him.

For the first time in days, Harper felt like she was lying with every silence.

Because she'd told herself she wouldn't sell him out.

But now, her career was hanging on whether or not she did.

***

The day slipped into late afternoon with very little said between them.

Harper sat at the writing table, eyes scanning the new draft of the lighthouse scene, but her mind wasn't absorbing the words. The weight of Celia's voice—sharp and clinical—still echoed in her ears.

Three days.

A statement.

Something public.

Or everything falls apart.

She'd worked too hard to lose her standing at the agency. She'd climbed her way to the top of a cutthroat industry by learning to wear ambition like armor—not letting people in, not making promises she couldn't deliver.

Except this time, she'd made a promise with more than just words.

She looked across the table at Elias. He was reading silently, a pen tapping rhythmically against the wood. His profile was softened by the afternoon light, that silver streak in his hair catching the sun just enough to make him look carved from memory. The man was frustrating, complex, and far more guarded than she had ever anticipated.

But he'd let her in.

Bit by bit.

And now she was the only person standing between his story and the industry he'd been running from for a decade.

And she was about to break him all over again.

Unless she told him first.

***

Later, as they wrapped up the scene and began packing up for the day, Harper moved slowly, deliberately. Her chest was tight, her thoughts racing.

She lingered at the window, watching the sun slip lower toward the horizon.

"Elias."

He looked up. "Yeah?"

She turned to face him. Her voice was calm, but her hands were cold. "There's something I need to tell you."

He set down his notebook and waited.

She stepped away from the window and sat back at the table, folding her hands over her knees. "My boss—Celia—called this morning."

He nodded once, but said nothing.

"She... she wants something to show for all this. Something publishable. A quote. An interview. Even a paragraph in your own voice. She's threatening to freeze the deal if we don't give them something by Friday."

The silence that followed wasn't tense—it was *absolute*. A vacuum.

Elias blinked slowly. "And when exactly were you going to tell me this?"

Harper swallowed. "I didn't want to pressure you."

"But you were going to?"

"I *am* telling you," she said. "I just... I wanted to find the right moment."

He laughed once, bitter and low. "You mean after I handed you something personal? After I trusted you with that page yesterday?"

Harper flinched. "This isn't about the agency. Not anymore. I'm not trying to sell you."

"But you *are*, aren't you?" he said sharply. "You came here with a contract and a deadline, and now that we've finally created something honest, you want to leverage it into marketing copy."

"It's not like that—"

"Then tell me what it's like."

She stood suddenly. "It's like watching someone crawl out of grief and realizing that you might be falling for him, and still knowing the world outside won't wait for that process to finish!"

Elias froze.

Harper's mouth hung open, the confession crashing out of her like a wave she hadn't seen coming.

They stood in the dim cottage light, two people who had bared everything *except* what mattered most—until now.

"You're falling for me?" he said, voice quieter now. The edge had softened, replaced with disbelief.

She looked down. "I don't know when it started. Maybe the second time you told me something real. Maybe the first time you didn't."

"And you didn't think that might make all this... harder?"

"I didn't come here to fall for you," she said. "I came here to finish a story."

"But now you're in it," he said.

And it wasn't an accusation.

It was a truth spoken aloud—one that didn't need defending.

Harper stepped forward. "I'll tell Celia no. I'll walk away from the agency if I have to. I'm not going to sacrifice this— what we've built—just to please people who've never read your words."

Elias's brow furrowed. "You'd walk away?"

"I've already come farther than I meant to."

For a long moment, he said nothing. Then his eyes dropped to the notebook in his hand—the one with the new, hopeful passage.

He passed it to her wordlessly.

She looked down at the open page.

Another new entry.

This one said:

> *She told the truth when it cost her.*
> *That's the only kind of story I still believe in.*

When she looked up, Elias was watching her with an expression she hadn't seen before. Not just admiration. Not just affection.

But *permission*.

Harper felt her throat tighten.

"I'm not asking you to go public," she whispered. "I'm just asking you to keep writing."

He nodded slowly. "Then let's write like no one's watching."

She smiled, her heart thudding in her chest. "Deal."

They didn't hug. They didn't kiss.

But something passed between them—something that didn't need punctuation.

Something that wasn't silence anymore.

It was *trust*.

***

That night, back at the inn, Harper emailed Celia two sentences:

> *This book isn't about branding.*
> *It's about healing.*
> *And if you try to force it, you'll lose the only story that still matters.*

She turned off her phone.

Closed her laptop.

And opened Elias's notebook instead.

Not to edit it.

But just to read.

***

Smoke and Mirrors

The morning after Harper's email to Celia, she woke feeling more weightless than she had in weeks.

The fog had lifted from the coastline overnight, revealing a sky so blue it looked almost surreal. The gulls outside called sharply, their wings slicing through the breeze like punctuation in the open sky. Harper pulled her sweater tighter around her shoulders and stood barefoot by her inn window, watching the waves crash below.

She'd taken a stand.

And she felt it.

The relief. The fear. The *rightness* of it.

But most of all, the lingering thrill of that final moment in Elias's cottage—his eyes locked with hers, that line in his notebook like an offering.

> *She told the truth when it cost her.*
> *That's the only kind of story I still believe in.*

She repeated it under her breath like a mantra as she packed her bag and headed out for the day.

***

When Harper arrived at the cottage, Elias was already at the writing table, fire crackling low behind him. He looked up and gave her the smallest smile—not just polite, but *warm*. Easy. Comfortable in a way that made her stomach flutter.

"Morning," he said.

"Morning." She dropped her bag on the chair and peeled off her coat. "You sleep?"

"Not much."

"Thinking or writing?"

"Both," he said. "But I made coffee, so at least one of those was productive."

Harper chuckled and poured herself a mug.

They spent the morning crafting a chapter where James returns to Evelyn's old house—now empty, abandoned, the paint peeling, the windows cracked. The metaphors wrote themselves, but Harper was surprised when Elias suggested adding a visitor: Evelyn's former neighbor, a woman in her seventies who recognized James instantly and spoke to him not with pity—but with anger.

"She blames him," Elias explained. "Not because he did something wrong—but because he disappeared. He let the silence do the talking."

Harper nodded slowly. "That's real."

"You'd be surprised how long silence echoes when you don't interrupt it."

The line stayed with her, even after the scene was finished.

***

After lunch, Harper stepped out to call Irene and check in on a package delivery—something she'd ordered from the bookstore back in the city. Irene answered with her usual clipped warmth.

"It's here," she said. "And so is something else. An envelope from your office. Marked urgent."

Harper stilled. "Did you open it?"

"I figured if someone's still sending you paper mail in 2025, they've got something to hide."

Harper forced a laugh. "And?"

Irene paused. "It's a copy of a contract. With your signature. And another I assume is his. Only…"

"Only what?"

"It's dated two weeks *before* you came here."

Harper's stomach dropped. "That's not possible. The only paperwork I signed was the pitch memo."

"Well," Irene said carefully, "this has a full ghostwriting clause in it. Legalese all over it. Looks like something someone wanted to make very real, very quietly."

Harper went cold.

Her pulse thundered in her ears.

"I'm coming now."

***

Twenty minutes later, Harper stood in the hallway of the inn, the envelope open in her hands.

She scanned the document line by line, her breath growing shallower with each paragraph.

Clause 4b: In the event that Mr. Elias Blackstone is unable or unwilling to complete a final manuscript, Ms. Harper Lane agrees to assume ghostwriting

duties to deliver a complete novel by deadline, at her discretion.

It was real.

And worse—it had her name on it.

She *hadn't* signed this.

But the signature at the bottom was hers. Scanned. Pasted. Forgery.

Her blood ran cold.

Celia.

It had to be her.

Celia had doctored the file—probably to protect the agency's investment, or to force a book out of Elias one way or another. If Harper had failed to get a manuscript out of him, they would've moved ahead using her words under *his* name.

Or so they'd planned.

And if Elias ever saw this...

Her stomach twisted violently.

It would confirm every fear he had.

That she wasn't here for *him*, or the story—but for the product. The deal. The lie.

Harper sank into the armchair near the window, the pages shaking in her hands.

She'd built trust with him piece by fragile piece.

This?

This could burn it all down in an instant.

***

Back at the cottage, Elias paced the writing room.

Harper had been gone for over an hour, and something about the way she'd left—rushed, pale, distracted—made the hair on the back of his neck bristle.

He moved to the table and picked up her notebook from earlier. She'd left it open to a scene they'd finished that morning. Her notes in the margins were softer now, more reflective. Gone was the sharp red ink of revision—replaced with soft pencil lines and the occasional phrase circled with a question mark.

She trusted the process now.

Trusted *him*.

Which is why the shift unsettled him.

He moved to the fire, staring into the flames. He remembered what she'd said the night before, the words that had stuck with him harder than anything she'd written:

> *"I'm not asking you to go public.*
> *I'm just asking you to keep writing."*

He *wanted* to trust that.

He *almost* did.

But the ghost of doubt lingered like smoke.

And he knew, in his gut, that something was about to change.

***

Harper's fingers hovered over her phone screen for a full minute before she finally tapped **Call**.

Celia answered on the second ring, all polished cheer. "So you've seen the package."

Harper's voice was cold. "Don't play coy with me. You forged my signature."

A beat. "I prefer *preemptively authorized on your behalf.*"

"Don't do that," Harper snapped. "Don't try to spin this like it's normal. It's illegal."

"Oh please," Celia said smoothly, "do you know how often contracts get 'massaged' in this business? We weren't forging a will. We were protecting the agency's assets—and yours."

Harper's knuckles whitened around her phone. "You signed me up to ghostwrite a book Elias wasn't even sure he wanted to write."

"And look at you now," Celia said. "He's writing. You're bonding. The story's happening. Everyone wins."

"No," Harper said sharply. "That's not how this works."

Celia's voice hardened. "You were supposed to get us a manuscript. You were supposed to keep him on schedule. The clause was insurance, Harper. In case he bailed."

"And what if he sees it?" Harper hissed. "What if he thinks I was in on it from the start?"

"Then you deny everything."

"I can't lie to him."

"Then you'll lose him. And us."

The words dropped like stones.

Celia softened her tone. "Harper, you've worked too hard for this career. You're good at what you do. But feelings don't sell books. Deadlines do."

Harper stared out the inn window, watching a single gull dive into the surf.

"I'm not ghostwriting his story," she said finally.

"Maybe not. But the moment he stops delivering, you will."

"No," Harper whispered. "I won't."

She ended the call.

Her hands were shaking, but her voice—finally—was not.

***

Back at the cottage, Elias returned from a short walk down to the beach, trying to clear his thoughts. The salt air had helped a little, but the quiet buzz of anxiety still hummed under his skin.

Harper hadn't come back.

And something in her voice before she left had felt... wrong.

Not rushed. Not distracted.

Afraid.

He went into the writing room, planning to straighten the notes they'd left out that morning. He paused when he noticed her messenger bag slouched near the door—still open, one corner of a folder sticking out.

He shouldn't.

He knew he shouldn't.

But something gnawed at him—something beyond curiosity. A sense of foreboding.

Elias crouched down and gently lifted the corner of the folder, enough to catch a single line of text on the visible page:

"Clause 4b: In the event that Mr. Elias Blackstone is unable…"

He froze.

Scanned the next few words.

"…Ms. Harper Lane agrees to assume ghostwriting duties…"

A sound escaped his throat. Not a word. More like the dull snap of breath colliding with disbelief.

He stood quickly, folder still in hand, his pulse thudding in his ears.

There was no date on the visible page. No signature. Just the clause.

But it was enough.

Enough to confirm the suspicion that had lived quietly in the corners of his mind since she arrived: that maybe she wasn't just here to help him write.

Maybe she was here to *write it for him.*

To profit off his grief.

To complete the myth of his comeback, even if it meant faking it.

He felt like the oxygen had been sucked from the room.

***

Harper returned to the cottage an hour later.

She stepped inside cautiously, calling out, "Elias?"

No answer.

She moved into the writing room and stopped cold.

The folder was on the table.

Open.

The page she feared most was on top.

Elias wasn't in sight, but his coffee mug had been shattered in the sink.

Harper's heart dropped.

She turned to find him standing in the doorway of the back room, arms crossed, face unreadable.

"Elias—"

"You should go."

Her stomach turned. "Please, just let me explain."

"I trusted you." His voice wasn't loud. That made it worse. "I let you in."

"I didn't sign that," Harper said quickly. "Celia did. She forged my name. I had no idea until today."

He said nothing.

"I confronted her. I told her I wouldn't be part of it. That I wouldn't write a word without you."

"You could've told me the minute you found it."

"I was going to."

"But you didn't." His jaw clenched. "You kept working. You let me keep opening up."

Harper stepped forward. "Because what we're building is real."

"How would I know that?" he said. "How would I *ever* know that now?"

She opened her mouth, but the answer didn't come.

Because she didn't know how to prove truth when the lie was already sitting there in black and white.

Elias picked up the folder, held it out to her. "Take this. And leave."

Harper's throat closed around the words.

"I'll come back tomorrow—"

"No," he said quietly. "You won't."

The room blurred at the edges as tears threatened. But Harper nodded, took the folder, and left the cottage in silence.

This time, it wasn't a creative pause.

It was heartbreak.

***

Harper didn't return to the inn. Not right away.

Instead, she drove aimlessly up the coastal road, her mind a mess of ash and fragments. The ocean was a blur beyond the cliffs, the steering wheel tight in her fists. Every mile she put between herself and the cottage felt both like a betrayal and a breath.

Elias's voice kept echoing in her head:

"You should go."

"How would I ever know what's real now?"

"No. You won't."

He hadn't yelled. He hadn't lashed out.

But he'd *shut her out*.

And somehow, that was worse.

She pulled over near a weather-worn overlook and parked the car. The wind was sharp here, biting through her coat. The sea below churned against jagged rocks, and for a moment, she imagined tossing the forged contract over the edge. Letting it disappear into the foam.

But that wouldn't change what had been said.

It wouldn't undo the broken trust.

And it wouldn't bring him back to the table.

Harper stood there until her fingers went numb, then slid back into the driver's seat and made her way—slowly—back to the inn.

***

Irene didn't say a word when Harper walked in.

Just handed her a cup of tea and pointed toward the chair by the fire.

Harper sank into it.

The warmth should have comforted her. It didn't.

She sat in silence until Irene finally lowered herself onto the couch opposite and folded her hands in her lap.

"I know that look," she said. "That's the face of someone who tried to tell the truth too late."

Harper stared into the fire. "He thinks I lied to him. That I played him."

"Did you?"

"No," Harper said quickly. Then, quieter: "Not on purpose."

Irene nodded. "Intent doesn't always matter when the wound's still bleeding."

Harper sipped the tea. It tasted like cinnamon and guilt.

"I should've told him the second I found the contract," she said. "But I was afraid. I didn't want to lose the progress we'd made."

"So you tried to protect it by hiding the very thing that could unravel it."

Harper looked up. "Isn't that what everyone does with love?"

Irene smiled sadly. "Only the ones who forget that trust isn't built in grand gestures. It's built in the moment you decide to say the hard thing. Even if it costs you the easy outcome."

Harper let the words sink in.

"I told him I didn't sign it."

"Did he believe you?"

"No. But I meant it."

Irene rose and walked to the small bookshelf behind the reception desk. She pulled a leather-bound volume and returned with it in hand. It wasn't a novel—just a plain journal.

She handed it to Harper. "You can't talk him back into trust. But maybe… you can write your way back."

Harper stared at the journal. "What if he doesn't read it?"

"Then you'll know you did the one thing he always said he respected."

Harper blinked. "What's that?"

"Told the truth. When it cost you."

***

At the cottage, Elias sat alone on the porch, the contract still folded in his lap.

He hadn't read past the first few lines.

Didn't need to.

The mere suggestion was enough.

She'd known.

She'd stayed.

She'd *worked* with him.

Even after learning she might have to finish the book in his name.

The fire crackled in the hearth behind him, untouched since Harper left. The house was quiet now. Too quiet.

James's voice echoed in his head—his fictional echo, that is. A man stuck in the past, whose only method of survival was silence and self-preservation.

He'd been writing that man for weeks.

He hadn't realized he was writing himself.

Elias picked up a notebook—*her* notebook. She'd forgotten it in the rush to leave. It was full of their scenes, her thoughts, and her own margins—personal, bold, vulnerable.

A line near the back caught his eye, circled twice in dark pencil:

"Some silences are built like walls. But others are doorways."

He closed the notebook and let out a shaky breath.

She hadn't faked her passion.

She hadn't faked the story.

But maybe she'd *feared* the consequences of her honesty—and he of his.

***

That night, Harper sat at the desk in her inn room, the journal Irene had given her open in front of her. She stared at the blank page for a long time before finally writing:

Elias,
I didn't sign that contract. I didn't know it existed until it was too late.
But I knew the moment I read it that it would destroy what we had if I didn't tell you.
And I still waited. That's on me.
I've spent most of my career hiding behind words that weren't mine. This is the first time I found one that felt like it belonged to me—to us. And I was terrified of losing it.
I don't want your story. I just want to be part of it.
If you never want to see me again, I'll understand. But I'll keep writing. Because some things are worth finishing.

She signed her name at the bottom.
Not as an agent.
Not as a writer.
Just:
Harper.

***

The morning sun broke across the cliffs in ribbons of pale gold, but the sea below was restless, wind-lashed, and dark. A sharp contradiction—not unlike the one twisting inside Harper's chest as she stepped out of her car in front of Elias's cottage.

She didn't knock.

She didn't call out.

She simply walked up to the front porch, placed the leather-bound journal on the wooden table beside the door, and stood there for a moment, her fingers grazing its cover one last time.

The front window reflected only her outline—blurry and unfinished.

"I'm sorry," she whispered, more to the house than the man inside it.

Then she turned and walked away.

No expectations.

No theatrics.

Just a single offering left behind, pages full of truth, pain, and the one thing she hadn't known how to give him before: her story.

***

Elias didn't open the door right away.

He'd heard her steps. Had seen her car.

Watched her from the shadows of the kitchen as she set something down—then turned and left without a word.

He didn't move until the sound of her engine faded completely.

When he finally stepped outside, he found the journal waiting like a quiet echo.

No note on top. No name.

But he knew what it was.

He brought it inside, laid it on the table, and stared at it for a long time.

He made coffee.

He paced the room.

He almost opened it three times.

And then finally, he did.

The words inside weren't structured like one of their scenes. They weren't meant for publication or critique.

They were just... **honest**.

Each line cut and healed in equal measure.

> *I didn't want your story. I just wanted to be part of it.*
>
> *If you never want to see me again, I'll understand. But I'll keep writing. Because some things are worth finishing.*

Elias set the journal down, his throat tight.

There was no performance in these pages.

Only **sincerity**.

Only Harper.

And he realized then that what had broken wasn't their story.

It was his fear that no one could care about him unless they could profit from his pain.

And Harper—despite all that had happened—had offered him her truth without asking for anything in return.

Not forgiveness.

Not absolution.

Not even a response.

She hadn't come to the door to beg or explain.

She'd left her words and walked away.

That was trust.

That was the pulse she'd talked about.

***

Later that afternoon, Elias opened one of the notebooks they'd used during their first few sessions together.

He flipped past scenes, ideas, arguments, and edits—past Harper's notes in the margins, her looping pencil scrawls that said things like *"too clean—let him bleed a little"* or *"this line hurts (which means keep it)."*

And near the back, he found a note he hadn't noticed before. Not in a scene, but on its own page:

> *James doesn't need to be saved.*
>
> *He just needs to remember he's still allowed to live.*

Elias stared at it for a long moment.

And then, quietly, he picked up his pen.

***

Flashback: Five years earlier.

The cottage was darker back then.

Dustier.

Silent.

Claire's absence had filled the space more fully than her presence ever had. The rooms were cluttered with untouched dishes, the linen-covered reading chair she'd loved, a bookshelf half-emptied after the fire. Her scent still lingered in the fibers of his old sweater.

Elias hadn't written in months.

Not a word.

113

Not even a note to himself.

The laptop stayed closed. The pen stayed dry. Because to write meant movement. And movement meant acceptance. And acceptance meant the final betrayal: admitting that she was gone and he was still here.

Back then, he thought silence would protect him.

But it hadn't.

It had only calcified the ache, made it permanent.

He remembered the night he tried to write again—one shaky sentence about a man waking up in a house that no longer knew him.

He'd torn the page out before it dried.

It felt too much like hope.

And hope, back then, was an insult.

***

Present Day

Elias stood in the doorway of the writing room, Harper's journal still open in his hands.

He could hear her voice in the words, even when they were silent.

And for the first time in years, he didn't feel like the house was haunted.

He didn't feel like he was, either.

There was a knock at the door.

Not Harper.

It was Irene.

She stood on the porch with a bag of groceries and a familiar, steady look in her eye.

"Figured you weren't eating," she said.

"I'm fine."

"You look like a man who's read something dangerous."

Elias cracked a small smile. "Maybe I have."

Irene stepped inside, placed the bag on the counter, and turned to face him. "She's not her boss. And she's not that contract."

"I know."

"She told me once she didn't believe in happy endings," Irene said. "But I think she believes in *true* ones."

Elias nodded slowly. "So do I."

"Good," Irene said. "Because I think you're the only one who can help her write one."

***

Harper didn't expect the knock at her door.

Not that night.

Not after the way she'd left his porch that morning—heart thrumming, nerves frayed, journal trembling in her hands like a white flag.

But there it was.

Two quiet taps.

She opened the door slowly, fully expecting to find Irene, maybe with a mug of tea or one of her wise metaphors wrapped in sarcasm.

Instead, it was Elias.

Standing on the porch, windblown, holding a single sheet of paper.

Not flowers.

Not an apology.

Just a page.

And somehow that felt more honest than anything else ever could.

His voice was quiet. "I rewrote something."

Harper didn't speak.

Didn't breathe.

Elias extended the page. "I think it's where we left off."

She took it slowly.

The paper was still warm from his hands.

He turned to go, but she caught his arm.

"Wait," she said. "Will you read it to me?"

Elias hesitated—then nodded.

She stepped back, opened the door wider, and let him in.

***

They sat by the window, cross-legged on the floor, knees almost touching.

Harper handed the page back.

Elias cleared his throat, voice barely above a whisper.

> *"James stood at the edge of the water, not waiting for the tide to go out—but waiting for the part of him that had been buried to rise again.*
> *Elise wasn't beside him this time. Not physically. But her words were.*

'You don't owe anyone your pain,' she had once said. 'But if you choose to share it, it becomes something else. Not a wound. A bridge.'

He finally understood what she meant.

Love wasn't a monument. It was movement. Forward, always forward—even when the past pulled like undertow.

And maybe the only way to survive wasn't to forget.

But to carry the story forward. Together."

Elias set the page down.

Harper blinked, eyes wet but not spilling over.

"James," she said softly, "has come a long way."

Elias nodded. "He had help."

She looked at him. "So did you."

He didn't look away. "I read your journal. Every word."

Harper held her breath.

"I know you didn't sign that contract," he said. "I believe you."

The tension that had lived in her shoulders for days—maybe longer—finally let go.

"I wanted to tell you right away," she said. "But I didn't know how."

"I know," he said. "I would've done the same."

She tilted her head. "You did, actually."

He smiled faintly.

Silence stretched between them—but this one wasn't strained.

It was *safe*.

A shared breath.

A recalibration.

Then Elias reached over and gently placed his hand over hers.

"I'm still writing," he said. "Not because I have to. Because I want to."

Harper turned her palm to meet his, fingers weaving through like ribbon.

"So am I," she whispered. "And I think… maybe we're not writing about James and Evelyn anymore."

"No," Elias said, eyes locked on hers. "I don't think we are."

***

The next morning, they sat across from each other at the cottage's writing table—not adversaries, not strangers, not even just collaborators.

But something warmer.

Something unnamed, but *becoming*.

The manuscript sat between them, its pages no longer just ink on paper.

Now it was proof—of healing, of hope, of what happens when you tell the story you were always afraid to.

Harper turned to the next blank page.

Elias dipped his pen.

And together, they began again.

Not with exposition.

Not with regret.

But with something far more rare:

118

Truth.

***

Margins of the Heart

The days that followed their quiet reconciliation passed in a kind of golden blur.

Not in the way of fantasy or infatuation, but in the quiet rhythm of two people finally moving in step. Harper and Elias wrote side-by-side at the wide oak table, the fire crackling, the sea beyond the windows no longer ominous, but familiar. Each scene they built became less like architecture and more like breath—organic, living, imperfect but deeply real.

Their characters changed, too.

James was no longer lost in memory. He still carried Evelyn with him—always would—but now his voice on the page held more curiosity than sorrow. Elise had softened, not into sentimentality, but into someone capable of hope. And the setting—once heavy with fog and silence—had begun to shimmer with moments of unexpected light.

Harper noticed it first in the dialogue.

> "Maybe we don't need to escape the fire," James said in one scene. "Maybe we just need to stop pretending it didn't burn us."

Elias had written that line.

And Harper had quietly circled it.

Twice.

***

One afternoon, they took their notebooks down to the bluff where the grass was wild and the cliffs sharp. The wind was strong, tugging at Harper's sweater, but the sun was warm on her cheeks. Elias sat beside her, scribbling in his own spiral-bound pad with a concentration that made her smile.

"Your handwriting changes when you're focused," she said.

Elias glanced over. "Changes how?"

"It gets taller. Straighter. Like you're trying to impress someone."

"Maybe I am," he said, not looking up.

Harper flushed, but didn't press.

Instead, she watched a gull ride the thermals overhead and asked, "When did you start writing again? Really writing. Not just for this project."

Elias paused, then lowered his pen.

"The night I read your journal," he said simply. "It reminded me why I started in the first place."

Harper felt the weight of that land in her chest like a stone—not heavy, but solid. Real.

"You wrote before the fire because of love," she said softly. "And now... you're writing because of it again."

He looked at her then—and held the gaze.

Neither of them said what hovered in the space between them.

But it was there.

A beginning not yet spoken.

***

That night, Harper stayed late.

They worked in tandem on a pivotal chapter—one in which James opens a box of Evelyn's belongings he's left untouched for months. Inside is a photograph of her laughing, barefoot in a summer dress, holding a letter she never sent.

The emotional tone of the scene was delicate—too easy to overplay, too tempting to understate. But Harper and Elias handled it like glass, offering suggestions gently, rewriting single lines until they found the right weight.

When it was finished, Harper read it aloud.

Elias watched her the whole time.

When she finished, neither spoke for a long moment.

Then he said quietly, "That might be the first thing I've ever written that didn't feel like bleeding."

Harper folded the page in her lap. "Maybe it's healing now."

He reached across the table and touched her hand.

It wasn't a grab. Not a pull.

Just a touch.

But it was enough.

Her breath caught.

She turned her palm to meet his, the same way she had days before, and this time, neither of them looked away.

The fire crackled behind them. The wind pressed gently against the windowpanes.

And for a moment, they weren't just author and agent, or co-writers, or even friends.

They were two people standing in the margin between what had been and what might still be written.

***

The next morning, the knock on the cottage door wasn't Harper.

It was Nina Templeton.

A senior VP from the publishing house.

Immaculately dressed in a slate-gray trench and expensive boots, she looked as out of place on the weather-beaten porch as a diamond in a tide pool.

Elias opened the door cautiously.

"Nina," he said flatly.

She smiled—polite, sharp. "It's been a long time, Elias."

He didn't invite her in.

She invited herself.

Inside, she peeled off her coat and looked around the cottage with appraising eyes.

"Charming, in a rustic, pre-war sort of way."

Elias said nothing.

Nina turned to face him. "So. You're writing again."

"Who told you that?"

She smiled. "Let's just say the literary grapevine has deep roots."

He frowned. "And you came all this way because...?"

"We'd like to be part of the comeback," she said simply. "The house wants first right of refusal. We're prepared to double the original offer. Maybe more."

Elias crossed his arms. "It's not about money."

"No, it's about legacy," she said. "And let's not pretend you didn't vanish when your last book became a cult classic. People still talk about *The Garden Below*. There's a whole subreddit."

123

Elias sighed. "I'm not interested in being a myth."

"Then let's make you real again," she said. "Visible. Celebrated. Read."

He was quiet.

Then: "This book isn't finished."

"But it will be."

"That depends."

Nina tilted her head. "On?"

"Whether you leave before Harper gets here."

***

Harper arrived at the cottage just after ten, a stack of revised pages in her arm and two lattes in a cardboard tray. She was smiling, lighter on her feet than she'd felt in weeks, the words from the night before still warm in her chest.

"I'm still writing. Because I want to."

"So am I."

She was beginning to believe that maybe, just maybe, they weren't just writing a book—they were writing *their* book. One filled with more than plot and character arcs. One layered with real emotion, scar tissue, and the impossible grace of second chances.

She didn't knock.

She never did anymore.

But the moment she stepped inside, the air changed.

Nina Templeton was standing by the fireplace, a mug in hand, looking as if she'd just stepped off a publishing conference panel.

Harper froze.

Elias was by the window, arms crossed, his expression taut and unreadable.

Nina smiled—too wide, too polished.

"Ah," she said, lifting her mug slightly. "The muse arrives."

Harper's heart sank. "What is she doing here?"

Elias didn't answer.

Nina gestured toward the table. "I came to discuss business."

Harper stepped fully into the room, setting down the coffee without taking her eyes off Nina. "You shouldn't be here."

"Neither should forged contracts, but here we are."

The words hit like a slap.

Harper stiffened. "That was Celia."

Nina's brow lifted. "Celia doesn't move without approval."

Harper blinked. "What do you mean?"

"I mean," Nina said, crossing to the window, "your agency didn't just act on desperation. They acted on opportunity. You were looped in, whether you admit it or not."

"That's not true."

"You really think your signature ended up on that clause by mistake?" Nina's voice lowered, silk turned to ice. "We've all seen you rise quickly, Harper. Quick climbs usually involve messy ladders."

"Get out," Elias said suddenly.

Nina turned, surprised.

"This is my house. You came uninvited. You insulted my co-writer. And you've made your intentions clear."

Nina narrowed her eyes. "You think she's innocent?"

"I *know* she is," Elias said.

"She's not the one who disappeared for ten years."

Elias stepped closer. "And I didn't come back to play the same games."

Nina smiled tightly, clearly recalculating. "Fine. I'll go. But know this—the industry is waiting. You can either return on your terms, or we'll write the story for you. Reclusive genius. Emotional breakdown. Shadow-drafted finale. You'll be a myth, Elias. One you won't control."

She turned to Harper. "And you'll be the footnote."

Harper's voice trembled with fury. "I'd rather be a footnote than a fraud."

Nina left without another word.

The silence that followed was dense.

Harper stared at the door for a moment after it closed, her lungs full of fire and disbelief.

Then she turned to Elias. "You believe me?"

He nodded slowly. "I read your journal. All of it."

She exhaled. "She made it sound like I was complicit."

"You're not."

"But -"

"I know," he said firmly. "I don't need her version of the story."

Harper looked away. "I hate that she could just show up and try to rewrite our narrative."

"She didn't rewrite it," he said. "She just reminded us why it matters."

They stood in silence for a moment. Then Elias took a step toward her.

"I'm not afraid of being forgotten," he said. "I'm afraid of writing something that doesn't mean anything. But with you…"

He trailed off.

Harper finished it for him.

"With me, it does."

***

That evening, they wrote side-by-side again.

The tension hadn't disappeared, but it had refocused—like two people building a wall not between them, but *around* what they were protecting.

They worked on a scene where James confronts a literary critic who misrepresents Evelyn's final novel—turning her quiet emotional masterpiece into a political weapon.

It was Elias's idea.

Harper suggested a line that made them both pause:

> *"You don't get to decide the story just because you read the last page."*

When she read it aloud, Elias looked over at her, his voice thick.

"Keep that," he said.

Harper smiled faintly. "I thought you'd say that."

***

They didn't talk much that night.

But they didn't need to.

Harper and Elias sat close at the long oak table, each working through their own pages, their own characters—yet somehow writing the same story.

The tension left behind by Nina's visit hadn't dissipated. It hung in the air like the scent of smoke after a fire. But it wasn't the suffocating kind. It was the kind that lingered as a reminder: *this matters.*

Elias broke the silence first.

"She's not wrong," he said quietly.

Harper looked up from her draft. "About what?"

"That the industry will try to own the narrative. If we don't define it ourselves, someone else will."

Harper nodded. "Then let's define it."

Elias met her gaze across the table.

Her voice was steady. "No ghostwriting. No handoffs. No half-truths."

He exhaled. "You want to go independent."

"I want to go honest," Harper said. "Whatever that looks like."

A flicker of something crossed his face—not fear, exactly, but reverence. Like someone hearing the exact thing they never thought they'd be allowed to want.

"You'd walk away from your agency?" he asked.

Harper nodded. "I already did."

Elias smiled faintly. "Then I guess I should finish writing this damn book."

Harper grinned. "We. We should finish writing it."

***

The next morning, they worked from the porch—a first.

A fog had rolled in off the sea, soft and slow, but the air was still warm enough to make the fresh coffee comforting instead of necessary. The gulls were quieter today, replaced by the low hum of waves and the occasional creak of the railing beneath their feet.

Harper flipped to a clean page in her notebook.

"We're almost at the end," she said. "James is coming back to the city."

Elias nodded. "And Elise?"

"She stays behind. At first."

"You think they separate?"

"No," Harper said softly. "I think they choose. Not out of need. Out of want."

Elias looked at her carefully.

"You're writing us," he said.

Harper didn't deny it. "We've been writing us the whole time."

He nodded slowly. "Then I guess we need to make the ending count."

***

The chapter they worked on that day took everything.

It wasn't flashy. There were no big twists. No car crashes or public declarations.

Just James walking through a bookstore—Evelyn's favorite—and finding a letter she had left for him, tucked behind the spine of a poetry book they once shared.

In the letter, Evelyn writes:

> *You don't owe me your grief. You don't owe me your guilt.*
> *What you gave me was love. What I give you now is the freedom*
> *to live again.*
> *Find someone who challenges you. Who sees the silence and stays*
> *anyway.*
> *That's how I'll know I didn't leave you with nothing.*

Elias had written that.

Harper couldn't read it aloud without her voice catching.

"You okay?" he asked gently.

She nodded, swallowing. "It's just… true."

Elias leaned back in his chair, watching her.

"Claire said something like that once," he murmured.

Harper looked up.

"She said if I ever fell in love again, she hoped it wouldn't be with someone like her," he continued. "She said I needed someone who could see through me. Not just around me."

Harper blinked, stunned. "She really said that?"

Elias nodded. "She said I needed someone who wouldn't let me hide behind words."

He met her eyes. "That sounds like you."

Harper's heart beat hard against her ribs.

She opened her mouth, unsure what would come out.

But Elias spoke first.

"After we finish this book," he said, "let's publish it ourselves. Tell the truth from the start. No agents. No houses. No positioning or spin."

Harper smiled. "No hiding."

He reached across the table and rested his fingers lightly against hers.

"No hiding," he repeated.

***

They wrote until the sun dipped below the edge of the sea.

Not everything was perfect. Some lines needed trimming. A few chapters still felt jagged. But the bones were strong. The characters were real. And the story—*their* story—was starting to hum with completion.

As they packed up for the night, Harper touched Elias's arm.

"I never thought I'd write something that mattered more than how it sold."

"You did," he said.

She smiled. "With you, I remembered how."

Elias looked at her then—long and quiet—and Harper thought for a moment he might kiss her.

But he didn't.

He just said, "Let's finish it."

And somehow, that was even more intimate.

***

They finished the book on a Tuesday.

The last paragraph came not with fireworks, but with stillness.

Harper had been scribbling ideas in the margin while Elias typed at the laptop. The windows were open, letting in the low rumble of the sea and the smell of salt. Somewhere outside, wind tousled the heather that lined the bluffs.

It was Elias who wrote the final line:

> *He didn't need to be rescued.*
> *He just needed someone who wouldn't turn away when the fire burned too bright.*

When he stopped typing, Harper looked up.

"That's it," she said softly.

Elias leaned back in his chair. "That's it."

They sat in silence for a moment, letting the weight of it settle—not the word count, not the chapters, but the truth inside it.

Harper reached across the table and placed her hand on the keyboard. "We did it."

Elias covered her hand with his.

"No," he said. "*You* did it. You pulled me back into this."

Harper looked at him. "We pulled each other."

The moment hovered again.

So many almost-kisses.

So many long glances.

But this time, Elias stood, walked around the table, and pulled her gently to her feet.

He didn't say anything.

He just leaned in and kissed her.

Soft.

Deliberate.

Like punctuation at the end of a sentence that had taken far too long to write.

Harper melted into it. She didn't overthink, didn't pull back—just let it happen, let the story fold into the space between them.

When they broke apart, their foreheads rested together.

"That was overdue," she whispered.

"About ten chapters overdue," he murmured back.

***

They spent the afternoon formatting the manuscript and double-checking final edits. Every now and then, their hands would brush. Elias would pass her a cup of tea. Harper would quietly fix a misplaced comma and tap the screen like it was a small joke between them.

It felt good.

Whole.

Finished.

But peace, as it often does, didn't last long.

Harper's phone buzzed around five p.m., screen lighting up with a text from Irene:

You should see this. Now.

Harper frowned and tapped the link Irene had included.

It opened a publishing gossip blog—*LitFuse*—known for scoops, scandals, and half-true headlines.

At the top of the page, in bold, was the title:

RECLUSIVE AUTHOR ELIAS BLACKSTONE'S "SECRET MANUSCRIPT" LEAKED—AND IT'S NOT HIS.

Harper's heart sank.

She scrolled quickly through the article. It contained:

- A detailed synopsis of the novel—from the lighthouse scene to the final paragraph.
- Quotes from "anonymous industry insiders" claiming Harper had ghostwritten the entire thing.
- A blurry photo of the notebook she'd left on the cottage table—open to her notes.
- A timeline suggesting Elias had handed her his story in exchange for "literary resurrection."

Harper's hands went cold.

"Elias," she said, voice shaky. "You need to see this."

He took the phone and read in silence.

His face didn't change—but that was worse.

The stillness. The way his jaw set.

"Where did they get this?" he asked finally.

Harper's voice was barely above a whisper. "I don't know. Only two people could've known the full synopsis—me and…"

She didn't finish.

Elias did.

"Nina."

Harper nodded. "Or Celia."

"But the photo," he said slowly. "That notebook. You left that here."

Harper blinked. "You think *I*—?"

"No," he said quickly, too quickly. "No. I don't think that."

But she could hear it—the *crack* of uncertainty beneath the words.

And it tore something open in her.

"I trusted you with everything," she said, her voice rising. "And one anonymous article has you doubting it again?"

"I'm not—" He stopped, running a hand through his hair. "I'm trying to understand how this got out."

"I *don't* know!" she snapped. "You think I'd sabotage the one thing I've ever built that actually matters to me?"

Elias didn't answer.

He didn't need to.

The silence did it for him.

Harper stared at him, throat thick, heart hammering. "You said we were writing this together."

"We were," he said. "We *are*."

"But you don't believe me."

He looked at her then—really looked at her—and the war on his face was clear.

Pain.

Regret.

Fear.

But the truth?

The truth was in his hesitation.

And Harper had seen enough of that already.

She took her bag, grabbed the printed manuscript from the table, and turned toward the door.

"Where are you going?" Elias asked.

"To protect our story," she said. "Even if you won't stand beside me to do it."

The door closed softly behind her.

But the break it left in the room was deafening.

***

The wind had picked up along the cliffs by the time Harper pulled into the inn's parking lot. She didn't go to her room. She didn't stop to speak to Irene. She went straight to the back office, locked the door behind her, and laid the manuscript down on the desk like it was an artifact.

Then she opened her laptop.

Her hands didn't tremble.

Her vision was clear.

She wasn't going to fight for permission. She wasn't going to wait for Elias to catch up. And she certainly wasn't going to let a leak from a bitter publishing exec define the story she had poured her soul into.

She opened her self-publishing account.

Created a new project.

Title: *Ink & Embers*

Author: *Elias Blackstone & Harper Lane*

She paused at the ampersand. Let her fingers hover.

She could've just listed Elias. Or herself.

But neither of those would've been the truth.

It was both of them.

Always had been.

She uploaded the manuscript.

Formatted the cover—a placeholder image for now, a lighthouse silhouetted against a sunset.

She chose a publication date for the following Friday.

Five days.

Long enough to prepare.

Short enough to make a point.

Then she sent a single email—to *LitFuse*.

Subject: The truth.

Message:

If you're going to write about our book, at least read the real one first.

Here's your exclusive:

Ink & Embers—out Friday.

Author's note included.

- Harper Lane

She hit **send**.

And finally—finally—leaned back in her chair and breathed.

***

Meanwhile, at the cottage, Elias stood alone in the writing room.

The silence was not comforting this time.

It was condemning.

The article still glowed on the screen of Harper's phone—which she'd left behind in her rush. The words now felt distant, exaggerated, hollow. Not because they didn't sting, but because he knew better.

He *knew* her.

Didn't he?

His doubt hadn't been about the leak.

It had been about *him*.

His own fractured trust. His pattern of pulling away. Of assuming loss before it happened. Of not believing he could ever hold something as steady and selfless as Harper.

She had offered him honesty. Repeatedly.

And what had he done?

Questioned her.

Again.

He crossed to the window, the waves crashing hard against the rocks below. The same cliffs where Claire's ashes had scattered years ago. The same cliffs he had nearly jumped from in his darkest hour—not to die, but to *stop remembering*.

But Harper had changed that.

She'd walked into his silence and stayed.

He picked up her phone.

Opened the most recent text thread: IRENE.

> *You okay? I'm with her now. She's setting the world on fire. In a good way.*

Elias smiled despite himself.

Then he saw the link Irene had sent—the draft of Harper's email to *LitFuse*.

> *Ink & Embers—out Friday.*

He opened the publishing dashboard on his laptop, found the placeholder listing, and saw it for himself.

Their names.

Their title.

Their story.

Live.

Together.

She hadn't erased him.

She'd given him *equal authorship*.

Elias sat down, opened a new document, and began typing an author's note of his own.

***

The next day, Harper walked into the indie bookstore on the edge of town—the same one Irene had introduced her to weeks earlier—and placed the manuscript in the hands of the owner.

"I want to do a small launch here," she said. "Nothing flashy. Just real."

The woman—Louise—flipped through the pages with reverence. "It's beautiful."

Harper smiled, nervous and proud. "We'll bring copies. There's a digital version too, but I want people to hold it."

"Of course."

"And," Harper added, "if a man named Elias Blackstone shows up, make sure he knows where to find me."

Louise raised an eyebrow. "Should I expect fireworks?"

Harper gave a half-smile. "Just embers."

Two days later, Harper stood in the back room of the bookstore, watching as the first box of paperbacks was delivered.

She ran her fingers along the spine.

Ink & Embers

By Elias Blackstone & Harper Lane

It felt *right*.

The weight of the book.

The title.

The truth of it.

She flipped to the author's notes.

Hers came first—a raw, confessional statement about fear, healing, and what it meant to write something you didn't want to sell—but needed to tell.

And then she saw his.

She hadn't known he'd added it.

It read:

> *I once believed stories could only come from pain. But I was wrong.*
> *This book came from something rarer—trust.*
> *Harper Lane didn't ghostwrite this novel.*
> *She gave it its pulse.*
> *And she gave me back my voice.*
> *This story is ours.*
> *And I would choose it again, and again, and again.*

Harper closed the book, her fingers trembling now.

Then the bell over the front door rang.

She didn't turn immediately.

She didn't need to.

She felt him behind her.

Felt the pause. The exhale. The *presence*.

Then Elias's voice, soft:

"You published it anyway."

She turned.

"I published *us*."

They stood in silence again—but now, the silence was full.

Full of the things they didn't have to say.

Full of what had already been written.

Elias stepped forward.

"I was wrong," he said. "About the leak. About you. About thinking I had to choose between protecting my story or trusting someone with it."

She didn't speak.

She let him finish.

"I want to be seen," he said. "And I want to be seen *with you*."

Harper swallowed hard. "Then stay."

He nodded. "I'm not going anywhere."

***

Ink Between the Lines

Two days after *Ink & Embers* released, it hit #7 on the Kindle Literary Fiction chart.

By day five, it had cracked the top five.

By day eight, it was trending on TikTok—not for any flashy stunt or influencer campaign, but because a quiet video of a young woman crying as she read the final chapter had gone viral with the caption:

> "I didn't know I needed to be forgiven for surviving until this book showed me how."

Then came the reviews.

Then the essays.

Then the speculation.

Who were the authors?

Was this truly Elias Blackstone's return—or something else entirely?

And who was Harper Lane?

The literary world had questions.

But neither of them answered.

***

The bookstore launch had been small. Intimate.

Just twenty chairs, a tray of wine and cheese, and a copy of *Ink & Embers* on every seat.

Harper had stood by the back shelves, trying to stay calm, when she felt Elias's hand on her lower back.

"You're shaking," he whispered.

"I'm fine."

"You lie better in prose."

She smiled despite herself.

"You don't have to speak," she said. "I know this kind of thing—"

"I want to," he interrupted.

She looked at him.

His voice softened. "For us."

***

Louise introduced them with a quiet reverence, telling the gathered readers that it wasn't every day a bookstore in a coastal town got to host a literary phoenix.

"And not just any comeback," Louise added. "But one that wasn't brokered by a publisher, a corporation, or a PR firm—but by two people who believed that the only story worth telling… is the one that almost never gets told."

Elias stepped up to the mic first.

He wore his usual navy sweater, slightly frayed at the cuffs, and spoke in a voice so even, it almost didn't sound like him.

"I spent ten years in silence.

Not because I ran out of things to say.

But because I stopped believing anyone would hear me if I said them.

This book changed that.

And so did the person who helped me write it."

He turned then, and looked at Harper.

And the crowd knew.

Without him saying her name.

Without her needing to stand.

The room broke into applause.

Harper swallowed the sudden emotion rising in her throat.

She hadn't expected to feel *seen* like this—not by readers, not even by Elias.

But in that moment, she wasn't Harper the agent.

She wasn't the fixer, or the middlewoman, or the safety net.

She was a writer.

A storyteller.

His *co-writer*.

And for once, that was more than enough.

***

The next day, the phone calls began.

Agents who had once ignored Harper now wanted to "circle back."

Editors who'd passed on Elias's prior drafts now begged for interviews.

Book clubs. Literary podcasts. Feature profiles.

Even **The New Yorker** sent an email with the subject line:

"Blackstone & Lane—Literary Alchemy or Marketing Genius?"

Harper stared at it and laughed.

She forwarded it to Elias.

His response:

Neither. Just grief, rewritten.

***

They spent the following week fielding offers they never asked for.

Movie rights. Translation deals. Exclusive interviews.

Harper rejected most of them outright.

"We don't owe anyone the whole story," she said, clicking delete.

Elias glanced up from his chair by the fire. "We already gave them the only one that matters."

Still, the attention stirred something uncertain in both of them.

What did it mean to protect something intimate in a world that wanted to devour it?

Where did the line fall between telling a story and *becoming* the story?

***

That Friday, a private email arrived from someone unexpected: Celia.

Subject: **You win.**

The body of the message was short.

Congratulations on the launch. If you'd led with this level of work, we might have found a more productive path together. Regardless, I'll step aside. You're clearly... a brand now. P.S. Nina's out. You're welcome.

Harper read it three times before passing her phone to Elias.

He raised an eyebrow. "This feels like a villain's resignation letter."

"She always had good timing," Harper muttered.

Elias handed the phone back. "You're not a brand."

She looked at him. "Aren't we? That's how they'll sell us."

"Not if we don't let them."

**

That night, Harper stood on the deck of the inn with a mug of tea and a manuscript in her arms—not *Ink & Embers*, but something new. A blank notebook, labeled only with a post-it that read: *Next*.

Elias joined her minutes later.

No jacket. No shoes. Just the chill of the sea air and the steady comfort of his presence.

"You okay?" he asked.

Harper shrugged. "I keep thinking about the book... not what we wrote, but what we left out."

"Like what?"

She looked out toward the dark horizon. "How we really met. What I was really running from. How many ways I almost ruined it."

Elias nodded. "Maybe that's the next book."

Harper turned to him. "You'd write with me again?"

He smiled. "There's still ink in the pen."

She leaned against his shoulder.

"I'm not afraid of being invisible anymore," she said.

He touched her hand.

"Good," he said. "Because I see you."

***

The email came on a Thursday afternoon, just as Harper was editing a second print run proof at the inn's front table.

Subject: *Keynote Invitation—Boston Writers & Storymakers Summit*

She read it once. Then again.

The message was direct, effusive. They wanted *her*—Harper Lane—to appear as a keynote speaker at the upcoming summit. Not Elias. Not the mysterious recluse or the ghost of literary legend.

Just her.

Her name.

Her story.

Her voice.

For a full minute, she didn't move.

It wasn't that she didn't feel honored. She did.

It wasn't that she didn't want to accept. She did that too.

But the invitation opened something that had stayed quietly folded between them since the book's release.

The world saw her now.

But did *he*?

***

That evening, Harper walked the short path to the cottage, clutching her laptop and a copy of the email. The sea air had

147

shifted again—colder, heavier—but she didn't notice. Her mind was full of paragraphs she hadn't written yet. Speeches she might give. And questions she wasn't sure how to ask.

Elias greeted her at the door with his usual half-smile and a folded paper towel in hand—he'd been staining the old window seat they'd begun converting into a reading nook.

"You brought your editor face," he said, nodding at the laptop.

Harper gave a tight smile. "Something came in."

They settled into their usual spots: Harper in the window chair, Elias on the edge of the table, a mug of coffee between them.

She handed him the invitation.

He read it silently, eyes scanning slower than usual.

When he finished, he set the page down gently.

"That's… big," he said.

Harper nodded. "They want me to speak about *Ink & Embers*. The creative process. The… partnership."

Elias rubbed his thumb along the rim of the mug. "Are they inviting me?"

She hesitated. "No. Just me."

He nodded, but Harper saw the flicker behind his eyes.

"I haven't answered yet," she said quickly. "I wanted to talk to you first."

"You should go," he said.

His tone was neutral. Too neutral.

Harper swallowed. "I'd rather we go together."

Elias looked away. "I'm not ready for panels. Spotlights. Hotel ballrooms full of people asking what grief taught me."

"Maybe it's not about them," Harper said gently. "Maybe it's about showing the world that we survived. That this story matters. That we matter."

He stood and crossed to the window, hands in his pockets.

"I spent ten years trying to disappear, Harper."

She stood too. "And you've spent the last two months coming back."

He was quiet.

"You said you wanted to be seen," she added.

"I do," he said. "But only by you."

Harper's voice softened. "I'm not asking you to become something you're not."

"No," Elias said, finally turning to face her. "But you're becoming something *you* are. And I'm not sure I fit into that version of your story."

Her chest tightened. "Don't do that."

"Do what?"

"Rewrite us before we've even finished the next chapter."

The silence hung too long this time.

Finally, Elias said, "You should accept the invitation."

Harper blinked back something bitter. "That's not an answer. That's permission."

"I'm proud of you."

"I didn't ask for pride," she said. "I asked if you'd stand beside me."

His answer came too late.

And too quietly.

***

149

Harper accepted the invitation that night.

Not out of spite. Not out of ego.

But because she'd made a promise to herself back when the pages were blank and the margins still wide:

She would never hide again.

***

The Boston Writers & Storymakers Summit was one of the largest literary events on the East Coast. Four days of panels, workshops, signings, and readings.

And Harper Lane was the closing keynote.

She arrived two days early and stayed in a boutique hotel just blocks from the conference center. Her badge, printed in bold serif font, read:

Harper Lane
Co-Author, Ink & Embers
Keynote Speaker

The first time she saw it pinned to her jacket, she had to sit down.

Not because she felt imposter syndrome.

But because for the first time in her career, she realized she wasn't hiding behind anyone else's name.

Not Celia's.

Not the agency's.

Not Elias's.

Just her own.

The keynote night arrived quickly.

The room was packed—four hundred writers, agents, editors, and aspiring storytellers.

When Harper took the stage, her legs were steady.

Her heart wasn't.

But she smiled into the light anyway.

"I used to think that stories had to be perfect to matter," she began. "That the work only counted if it was polished, pristine, complete. But then I met someone whose silence was more honest than most people's confessions. And together, we wrote something imperfect. Raw. Grief-laced. Hope-stitched. And it changed us."

A pause.

A breath.

"And here's what I learned: The most important story you'll ever write… is the one you're terrified to tell."

The applause thundered.

But even as it echoed through the ballroom, Harper looked out into the crowd and saw the one empty chair she'd left open in the front row.

He wasn't there.

And somehow, that hurt more than all the praise could soothe.

***

Harper didn't expect fireworks when she returned to the cottage.

But she also didn't expect silence.

The front door was unlocked, the lights dim, and the scent of salt air clinging to every surface. A cup sat abandoned on the table, half-full. Elias's coat was still hanging by the door. His shoes were tucked neatly by the mat.

Everything in place.

Except *him*.

She found him in the writing room, seated at the desk, staring at a blank screen. Not typing. Not editing. Just sitting— as if he were waiting for something to move inside him again.

He didn't turn when she entered.

"You weren't at the summit," she said.

"I know."

"You said you were proud of me."

"I still am."

"But you couldn't show up."

Elias exhaled, voice low. "I didn't want to be the man in the shadows. Watching you shine."

Harper crossed her arms. "Then be the man *beside* me."

He turned, finally meeting her gaze.

"I don't know how."

"Yes, you do," she said softly. "You do it every time we sit at this desk. Every time we argue about commas. Every time you choose a word that says what you're afraid to say out loud."

He looked away.

Harper stepped closer.

"You told the truth on the page," she said. "But the story doesn't end there. It keeps going—outside the margins. In real time. And right now, you're writing a version of yourself that stays hidden."

Elias stood abruptly, pacing.

"You don't understand -"

"I *do!*" she snapped. "I understand what it means to be terrified of being seen. To wonder if the version of yourself you've stitched back together is strong enough to hold under the weight of someone else's gaze. I know that fear. I lived it."

He stopped pacing.

"You walked away from that," he said.

"I walked *through* it."

They stood in tense silence, the distance between them more emotional than physical.

Finally, Harper softened.

"I don't need you to stand on a stage, Elias. I don't need you to give interviews or sign books. But I need you to stop treating yourself like a ghost."

His eyes glinted. "I spent ten years becoming one."

"Then come back," she said. "Not for me. For you."

He stared at her.

Long enough for her hope to falter.

Then, quietly, he said, "I kept the chair empty."

Harper blinked. "What?"

"At the summit. You left a chair open. I saw it in the photo."

He reached into a drawer and handed her a printout—a screengrab from the event's livestream. Her on stage. A single empty seat in the front row.

Elias's voice was raw now. "I watched. From here."

"You watched me speak?"

He nodded. "I couldn't be there. But I needed to hear you."

Harper looked down at the image. At the seat. At the way he had seen her from the shadows—and chosen to witness anyway.

She met his eyes. "Next time, sit in the damn chair."

He cracked a small smile. "That an order?"

"It's a page break," she said. "Not the end."

***

Later that night, Elias did something Harper hadn't seen him do since the day they met.

He opened a blank document.

Not on their joint project.

Not a revision.

Not a memory.

But something new.

Untitled.

His own voice.

Raw. Present. Alive.

He looked over his shoulder at her, standing in the doorway.

"I don't know if I remember how," he said.

Harper crossed the room, leaned over him, and kissed the top of his head.

"You do," she whispered. "Just don't edit as you go."

He smiled—small, but true—and began to type.

***

The essay went live on a Sunday morning.

No fanfare.

No announcement.

Just a quiet post on a literary blog that had once published Elias's earliest short stories under a different name.

The title was simple:

What I Didn't Say the First Time

The byline was unmistakable.

By Elias Blackstone

In less than twelve hours, it was shared over 30,000 times.

***

Harper read it at the kitchen table of the inn with a cup of black tea and her heart in her throat. The piece was barely 1,500 words—spare, elegant, and devastating.

> *I stopped writing after the fire because I thought silence was the only way to honor what I'd lost.*
> *But silence becomes a grave if you lie in it too long.*
> *I met someone who didn't try to fix me. She just stood still long enough for me to stop running. And in that stillness, I heard my own voice again.*

The essay ended with this:

Grief didn't end when I put down the pen.

It ended when I picked it up again—and found someone sitting across from me.

Harper finished reading and had to blink back tears.

He hadn't just come back to the world.

He'd come back whole.

***

By Monday, the inbox she and Elias shared for *Ink & Embers* was flooded.

Requests to reprint the essay.

Offers for speaking engagements. Op-eds. Podcasts. International rights.

But one email stood out.

From a name she hadn't heard in months.

Zoe Mansfield—senior editor at **Westminster House**, one of the Big Five publishers.

Subject: *Let's talk about the next chapter… and your legacy.*

Harper read the email twice before she brought it to Elias.

They were sitting in the sunroom, him barefoot, her editing page proofs for a foreign translation.

"Zoe Mansfield emailed," she said.

Elias looked up. "Who?"

"Westminster House."

His eyebrows lifted. "We queried them two years ago."

"She wants to repackage *Ink & Embers*."

He stared. "Repackage how?"

"Hardcover. Audiobook. Deluxe edition. A foreword by a Pulitzer winner. Anniversary launch. Full marketing campaign."

Elias didn't react at first.

Then: "She read it?"

"Yes."

"And liked it?"

"She said it made her cry."

He smiled faintly. "Okay, well. I guess that's a start."

Harper hesitated.

"There's one catch."

Elias met her eyes.

"They want to retitle it."

Elias blinked. "What?"

"She said it's too 'subtle for the market.' She suggested something... more emotional. *The Fire We Survived.* Or *Letters After the Burn.*"

Elias frowned. "That's not the story."

"I know."

"They want a trauma story."

"They want to sell pain."

Harper closed the laptop. "I said I'd discuss it with you. But I don't want it. Not like that."

Elias sat back, rubbing a hand across his jaw.

"It's tempting," he admitted. "To reach more readers. To tell Claire's story to more people."

"But not at the cost of ours," Harper said.

He looked at her.

Soft.

Steady.

"Then we don't."

***

That evening, they walked the bluff behind the inn—the same path Harper had wandered alone when she first arrived in the coastal town with nothing but a contract and an impossible assignment.

Now she walked it with someone who saw her.

Really saw her.

She took his hand.

"I've always known how to sell stories," she said. "It's what I was trained to do. But this one… I want to keep it. Not hide it, not hoard it—but keep it *ours*."

Elias looked out at the darkening sky. "You think we can?"

"Yes," she said. "As long as we remember who we wrote it for."

He squeezed her hand. "Each other."

***

The next day, Harper responded to Zoe's email.

> Thank you for your interest in *Ink & Embers*. We appreciate your admiration and enthusiasm for the story.
>
> However, the book we published is the book we meant to write.
>
> Not a brand. Not a product.
>
> A pulse.

That doesn't get repackaged.

Sincerely,

Harper & Elias

Then she shut the laptop and went back to writing.

Not an email.

Not a pitch.

Just words.

The next story.

Because that's what storytellers do.

Even after the embers cool.

Even after the pages close.

They begin again.

***

Louise set out the candles just as the sun dipped below the waterline.

She didn't believe in overhead lighting for readings—too harsh, too sterile. Instead, she placed tall glass votives along the bookshelves and windowsills, giving the room a soft, golden warmth that felt like memory.

Harper sat cross-legged on a love seat near the center of the store, watching the guests trickle in. Most were locals. A few had driven in from Portland or Boston. One woman said she'd flown from Texas.

All of them carried *Ink & Embers* in their hands.

Marked-up. Dog-eared. Loved.

Elias sat beside her, surprisingly calm.

He wore a slate button-down and his old scuffed boots. His hair had been finger-combed, but a strand still fell across his forehead in defiance. He didn't try to fix it. He never did.

He turned to her as the room filled.

"Nervous?" he asked.

Harper smiled. "Strangely… no."

"Because of me?"

"No," she said. "Because of us."

***

Louise welcomed everyone with her usual dry wit.

"Tonight isn't a reading," she said. "It's a conversation. These authors didn't just give us a novel. They gave us a mirror. And I suspect some of us saw ourselves in it. That deserves something quieter than applause."

The room hummed with agreement.

Then Harper and Elias stepped up to the makeshift stage— a wooden riser flanked by two floor lamps—and sat on a pair of mismatched chairs.

Harper held the mic first.

"I've worked in publishing a long time," she began. "Long enough to know that sometimes, the best stories aren't the ones that shout. They're the ones that whisper—across pages, across rooms, sometimes across grief."

She looked at Elias.

"I met Elias because I was sent to convince him to write again. What happened instead was… we wrote each other back into being."

She handed him the mic.

Elias took it without hesitation.

"I used to believe writing was extraction. Pulling from the wound. Bleeding onto the page," he said. "But then Harper taught me that writing can also be building. Stitching. Holding."

He looked down for a moment, then back at the audience.

"And sometimes, when you tell a story you think no one else will understand… someone across the room whispers, 'Me too.'"

There wasn't applause, just a quiet swell of breath.

Someone sniffled.

Someone else pressed a hand to their chest.

And that was enough.

***

During the Q&A, a reader in the front row raised her hand.

She looked to be in her sixties. Silver braid. A paperback held like scripture.

"Did you know," she asked, voice trembling slightly, "how much this story would mean to people like us? The ones who thought it was too late to love again?"

Elias glanced at Harper.

"No," he said. "But I knew it wasn't too late to try."

The woman nodded, wiping at her cheek. "Thank you."

Later, another reader asked about the writing process.

"How did you split the work? Who wrote what?"

Harper grinned. "We fought a lot."

Elias added, "We kissed more."

Laughter rippled through the room.

"But seriously," Harper said, "we wrote the scenes that scared us. That's how we knew they mattered."

Elias nodded. "And then we rewrote them… together."

***

After the event, they signed copies.

Names. Notes. Inside jokes.

One reader asked Elias to inscribe hers with *something personal,* so he wrote:

> *For the ones who survived the fire—and still chose to build.*

When the last book was signed, and the last reader had thanked them, Harper gathered her bag and looked toward the door.

But Elias didn't move.

He stood in the center of the bookstore, hands in his pockets, eyes still scanning the room.

"Are you okay?" Harper asked.

He turned to her slowly.

And then he said it.

Clearly. Unshaken.

"I love you."

She blinked.

Not because she didn't know.

But because he'd never said it aloud.

"I've written it a hundred times," he said. "But I needed to say it."

Harper crossed to him. Took his hand.

"I know," she whispered. "I love you too."

No crowd.

No applause.

Just candlelight.

Just them.

And it was enough.

***

That night, back at the cottage, Elias placed a new notebook on the table.

Blank.

Unlabeled.

He slid it toward Harper.

Her eyebrows rose. "What's this?"

"A beginning," he said. "Again."

She opened it.

Inside, on the first page, he had written in his familiar, tall handwriting:

Chapter One: This time, we're not afraid.

***

Writing the second book was supposed to be easier.

It wasn't.

For the first three weeks, Harper and Elias sat across from each other with coffee mugs and open notebooks, just like before. But the rhythm wasn't there.

The silence between them wasn't collaborative—it was cautious.

As if they were waiting for the other to speak first, to break the fragile peace that success had imposed on their creative process.

"Why can't we just start?" Harper asked one morning, her pencil resting untouched on the legal pad beside her laptop.

Elias shrugged. "Because now we're not just writing for ourselves."

She looked at him. "You mean the readers."

He nodded. "And the press. And the industry. And the expectations."

She sat back in her chair. "We didn't care about any of that before."

"That's because we didn't know it would matter."

***

The pressure didn't come from one place—it came from *everywhere*.

Fans begged for a sequel. Publishers sent offers Harper politely but consistently declined. Literary blogs speculated about what Elias and Harper would write next.

Some said *Ink & Embers* was lightning in a bottle—impossible to follow.

Others said their relationship was "the real narrative," and the next book would prove whether it had been a fluke or a foundation.

Harper hated the word **fluke**.

Elias hated **foundation** even more.

Because what if the next story wasn't built right? What if they cracked it open before it had a chance to live?

***

One afternoon, they sat by the fireplace, outlines scattered across the coffee table.

"So what do we actually *want* this story to be?" Harper asked.

"Something different," Elias said.

"How different?"

He paused. "No lighthouses. No fires. No mourning lovers."

Harper tilted her head. "A comedy?"

He cracked a smile. "Maybe."

"A heist novel?"

"Too much research."

Harper reached for a pen. "What if it's just... two people trying to figure out what love looks like when no one's watching?"

Elias's smile faded into something softer. "Now that sounds terrifying."

She raised her eyebrows. "Which means it's probably the right story."

***

Still, progress was slow.

They wrote one chapter in a week.

Then rewrote it.

Then scrapped it.

The words didn't move the way they used to. Not because the connection was gone—it wasn't—but because everything around the writing had changed.

The cottage was no longer a retreat.

It was a place of expectation.

Elias caught himself second-guessing every sentence. Harper started saving three versions of every draft.

And neither of them could quite admit it aloud:

They were scared.

Not of failing.

But of writing something that would matter less than the first time.

***

At the end of one particularly fruitless writing day, Harper tossed her notebook aside and stood.

"I think I need a break."

Elias looked up. "From the book?"

She hesitated. "From *this*."

He nodded slowly, trying not to look disappointed. "Okay."

Harper softened. "Not forever. Just… a weekend. I'll go visit my sister in Boston. Clear my head."

Elias stood too. "I get it."

They hugged.

It wasn't cold. It wasn't distant.

But it wasn't quite the warmth of before.

And that, more than anything, unnerved her.

***

Harper left the next morning, promising to call.

Elias watched her car disappear down the long gravel drive, then returned inside and sat alone at the table.

The empty seat across from him stared back like a blank page.

***

The Story After the Ending

Boston felt louder than she remembered.

Or maybe Harper had grown quieter.

The clatter of the T, the caffeinated buzz of sidewalk conversations, the sharp angles of downtown buildings—it all made her feel like a character dropped into the wrong scene. She'd only been gone a few months, but the version of her that had lived here—Harper the agent, Harper the fixer—felt like a story she had outgrown.

Still, when she met her sister Jess at their usual café near Back Bay, it was easy to slip into old rhythms.

"You look rested," Jess said, stirring oat milk into her latte.

Harper smiled. "Do I? I feel like a slow-brewing nervous breakdown."

"Your version of rested, then."

They laughed.

Over croissants and cappuccinos, they talked about the book launch, the coastal town, Elias. Jess listened without interruption as Harper described the strange beauty and the strange pressure of their post-publication life.

Then Jess asked the one question Harper had been avoiding:

"Do you want to write another book with him?"

Harper stared at her mug.

"I want to write *a* book," she said carefully. "I'm just not sure what we're writing anymore."

Jess didn't press. She never did.

But that silence made the question louder.

***

Later that afternoon, Harper ducked into the lobby of her old agency's building—not to return, not to grovel—but because she had agreed to coffee with a former colleague: Mara Sloane.

Mara had been one of the only people who didn't abandon Harper during the Celia fiasco. She'd reached out after *Ink & Embers* had gone viral, but Harper hadn't replied then.

Now, curiosity outweighed caution.

They met in the café on the building's ground floor.

Mara still wore tailored blazers and subtle gold jewelry that whispered power. But her smile was genuine.

"You look better than your last author photo," Mara said, sitting down.

"That's a low bar."

Mara laughed. "You want the praise or the pitch first?"

Harper raised an eyebrow. "Let's start with honesty."

Mara leaned in.

"You've built something rare, Harper. You broke away from a toxic agency, found your voice, helped Elias Blackstone come back from the dead, and wrote a bestselling literary novel. That's not luck. That's *talent*."

Harper said nothing.

"So here's my pitch," Mara continued. "Come write a solo novel. Under your name. On your terms. No ghostwriting. No partnership. Just you."

Harper blinked. "You want me to leave the book I'm co-writing with Elias and… start a new one?"

169

"I'm saying," Mara said, lowering her voice, "maybe that story's already told."

Harper leaned back.

The idea sat uneasily in her stomach—not because she couldn't do it. She *could*. She had ideas, notebooks, scraps of dialogue that didn't belong to anyone but her.

But the thought of leaving Elias behind in the margins?

That didn't sit quietly.

"I'll think about it," Harper said.

Mara nodded, already satisfied. "That's all I ask."

***

Back in her hotel room that night, Harper reread the proposal Mara had sent.

A generous advance.

A debut under her own name.

Full creative control.

The offer was everything she'd once believed she wanted.

But now, her fingers hovered over the *reply* button like it was a detonator.

She didn't send anything.

Instead, she picked up her phone and stared at Elias's contact photo—the one she'd taken during their first walk on the beach, wind-blown and brooding, the sun a faint halo behind him.

She started typing.

Miss you.

Hope the sea hasn't swallowed you up.

No reply came right away.

And that, more than the offer, unsettled her.

***

Back at the cottage, Elias hadn't touched the new manuscript.

Instead, he'd returned to an old ritual: long walks through the woods behind the house, journal tucked into the crook of his elbow, silence as his only company.

He wasn't avoiding the work.

He was avoiding *why* it suddenly felt so heavy.

Every page reminded him of something he hadn't admitted yet—not even to Harper.

He was afraid their story had already peaked.

That the honesty of *Ink & Embers* had been a singular moment in time, born of grief and connection and surprise.

And now, without surprise, what was left?

Routine?

Expectation?

Love?

He wasn't sure if he could write from a place of *stability*.

He'd only ever known how to write through pain.

He opened his journal and scribbled:

> *What if joy isn't a muse?*
> *What if love dulls the edge I used to carve my name into the world?*

Then he closed the notebook.

And stared out at the waves, asking a question he didn't
know how to answer:
Is this what it means to be happy?
Or is this what it means to be safe?

***

The drive back from Boston was quiet.

Harper played no music. Took no calls.

Her thoughts were a symphony of imagined reactions,
rehearsed explanations, and worst-case scenarios. Elias would
be upset. Hurt. Maybe angry. She tried to find a version of the
conversation where it ended in peace, but each possibility felt
like writing the end of a chapter she hadn't meant to start.

By the time she pulled up to the cottage, the air was thick
with fog and salt and the kind of stillness that didn't feel
peaceful—just unspoken.

Elias was on the porch, barefoot, mug in hand.

He stood when he saw her, a flicker of relief in his
expression.

"You came back," he said.

Harper stepped out of the car. "I said I would."

He nodded once, then motioned toward the door. "You
want coffee? Tea?"

"No," she said. "I want to talk."

He led her inside without a word.

***

They sat across from each other in the writing room, the same place they had finished *Ink & Embers*, the same table where every confession had slowly unraveled between them.

"I met with someone in Boston," Harper said. "An editor."

Elias nodded slowly, eyes unreadable. "Okay."

"She offered me a solo book deal."

Still no reaction.

"She wants to publish me. Under my name. No co-writer. Full control."

Elias leaned back in his chair. "Did you say yes?"

"No," Harper said. "But I didn't say no either."

He didn't speak for a long time.

Finally, he asked, "Why didn't you tell me before you went?"

"I was afraid it would feel like a betrayal."

"Does it?"

Harper looked down. "A little."

Elias exhaled through his nose, not angry—just quiet.

"I'm not surprised," he said.

That stopped her.

"What do you mean?"

"I mean," he said, "you're brilliant. And you don't need me to write a great book."

"That's not the point."

"Isn't it?" he asked gently.

Harper felt the sting behind his words, not because he was accusing—but because he wasn't.

He was letting go.

Too easily.

"Are you… okay with this?" she asked.

"I don't want to lose what we built," Elias said. "But I also don't want to be the reason you stop becoming who you're meant to be."

Harper blinked. "So you think we can't write together and still grow?"

"I think," Elias said, "that we wrote a masterpiece out of pain and surprise. And now that we're trying to write out of routine… we don't know how."

She stared at him. "So that's it?"

"No," he said. "That's *honesty.*"

***

They didn't fight.

That was the strange part.

They sat in the stillness, holding the soft, fragile edges of something that had once been invincible—a collaboration born in fire, now faced with the quiet, slow erosion of pressure and expectation.

"I love writing with you," Harper said finally.

"I love *you,*" Elias replied.

Her heart skipped.

"I know," she said. "But what if that love isn't enough to keep the story going?"

Elias looked at her, his expression tender. "Then maybe the next story isn't *ours* to write together. Maybe it's just… ours to carry."

Tears pressed at the corners of her eyes.

Not from heartbreak.

From the impossible gentleness of being loved without being owned.

***

Later that night, Harper found a note on her side of the writing table.

Elias's handwriting, familiar and even.

> *Whatever you choose—your name, your book, your voice—I will read every word.*
> *And I'll know where they came from.*
> *From fire.*
> *From ink.*
> *From us.*

She folded the note, tucked it into the back of her journal, and lit a single candle.

No laptop.

No deadline.

Just a blank page.

A new beginning.

Maybe alone.

Maybe not.

But honest.

Always honest.

***

Harper waited three days before replying to Mara's email.

Not because she was unsure.

But because this time, she wanted to choose slowly.

Deliberately.

Without fear.

Without needing permission.

She sat on the porch of the cottage with her laptop balanced across her knees, the sea wind tangling her hair, Elias somewhere inside, humming along to an old jazz record.

This was not the end of something.

It was the *evolution* of something.

A truth she hadn't been ready to face until now.

She clicked *Reply*.

> Mara,
>
> Thank you for the offer. After careful thought, I've decided to move forward—not because I'm walking away from what I built with Elias, but because I finally understand I have stories that are mine to tell alone.
>
> But you should know:
>
> I wouldn't have found this voice without him.
>
> Harper

She hit send.

No panic.

No regret.

Only clarity.

***

That evening, she told Elias on their walk along the cliffs.

"I said yes," she said.

He didn't ask what she meant.

He already knew.

He nodded. "Good."

"You're not upset?"

"No," Elias said. "Because now I get to be your first reader."

She smiled. "You've always been more than that."

They stopped near the edge of the bluff.

The sea below was wild tonight, foaming and full of motion.

Harper reached for his hand.

"I don't want to stop writing with you. Even if it's not books."

Elias looked at her, eyes warm and clear.

"We're still telling a story," he said. "It just doesn't always have to be one we bind and sell."

***

The next few weeks took on a new rhythm.

Harper worked on her solo manuscript at the inn's sunlit corner table, surrounded by locals who still treated her like one of their own.

Elias spent his mornings drafting short essays and poetry, slowly submitting them to small literary journals.

They still read each other's work.

Still offered edits.

Still argued—gently—about word choice and pacing and whether a comma could ruin a line.

But the urgency was gone.

The pressure.

The noise.

What remained was trust.

Respect.

And an ease that felt earned.

***

One afternoon, Harper returned to the cottage to find Elias on the porch, typing furiously.

"Something good?" she asked.

He looked up, his expression caught somewhere between embarrassment and pride.

"A piece about us."

"Us?"

"Sort of. It's about writing a story with someone who taught you how to live outside of it."

Harper sat beside him.

"Will you publish it?"

"I might," he said. "Or I might just give it to you."

She leaned on his shoulder. "I'll take it either way."

***

That night, Elias handed her a printed page.

No title.

No byline.

Just the first line:

We wrote one book together—but we built a life in the margins.

Harper didn't cry.

She just folded the page, kissed him once, and whispered, "Let's keep writing."

***

Harper finished the first draft of her solo novel in the quiet hours of a late September evening, long after the inn had gone dark, long after the coastal breeze had stilled outside the windows.

She didn't feel triumphant.

She felt... relieved.

She printed the last page, stacked the manuscript neatly, and ran her fingers over the title page.

It read:

By Harper Lane
To the one who taught me how to tell the truth and live with it.

She didn't have to name him.

Elias would know.

***

When she returned to the cottage the next morning, Elias was on the porch, reading one of her earlier drafts—his coffee half-drunk, his expression unreadable.

She waited.

He set the pages down slowly and looked at her.

"It's bold," he said.

She braced herself. "Too bold?"

"No," Elias said. "It's yours. Entirely. And that makes it the best thing you've ever written."

She blinked. "You really think so?"

"I do."

He stood, crossed the distance, and took her hands.

"It doesn't feel like the kind of story you had to write. It feels like the one you were *meant* to write."

She exhaled, deeply.

That was all she'd needed to hear.

***

As the weeks passed, the manuscript made the rounds.

Mara handled it with care, pitching it not as a "companion to *Ink & Embers*," but as Harper's true debut.

It didn't need Elias's name to hold weight.

It didn't need a tragedy at its center to be meaningful.

It was about resilience.

About reinvention.

About the kind of love that didn't save you, but let you become someone worth saving yourself for.

By December, three publishers were bidding.

Harper chose the smallest one.

The one that promised craft over campaign, reader over trend, and integrity over hype.

And Elias?

He celebrated with a quiet dinner at the cottage—her favorite meal, her favorite candle, and a card that simply read:

You wrote your way home.

***

The press didn't understand the shift at first.

They had latched onto the Elias-and-Harper duo as the mysterious literary pair of the year.

When Harper's book was announced as a solo effort, speculation churned.

"Are they splitting?"

"Was the magic a one-time thing?"

"Was *Ink & Embers* an emotional affair in literary form?"

They ignored it all.

Because while the headlines flailed, Harper and Elias kept building something even the critics couldn't define:

A life that didn't depend on sharing every page.

A partnership built on permission and space.

***

They still wrote together, occasionally.

A short story here.

An article there.

But mostly, they wrote beside each other.

Two desks.

Two screens.

Two minds.

One rhythm.

Sometimes Elias would hand her a single paragraph for feedback.

Sometimes she would read a passage aloud and ask, "Too vulnerable?"

He'd say, "Not enough."

And she'd rewrite it with more blood, more breath, more truth.

That was their new collaboration.

That was enough.

***

Months later, Harper's book hit shelves.

A slim hardcover with a black-and-white cover—no author photo, no bold promises.

Just a title in clean serif font:

What We Keep Quiet

Inside the jacket, a simple dedication:

To those who outgrow silence.
And the ones who wait beside them while they do.

***

At the launch party in a small Boston venue, Harper read a passage to a room of fifty.

Not five hundred. Not televised.

Just people.

Just readers.

And Elias, standing quietly near the back with a drink in hand, pride stitched across his face in a way words could never reach.

When the reading ended and people swarmed to ask questions, Elias stayed back.

He didn't need the spotlight.

He'd already had his scene.

Now, he was watching hers.

And loving every minute of it.

***

That night, in the quiet of their shared bed, Harper turned toward him and whispered, "Thank you."

"For what?"

"For letting me go… and never making me feel like I had to leave."

Elias ran his hand gently down her arm.

"I didn't let you go," he said. "I just stopped holding the pen for you."

She kissed his shoulder. "I think that's the most romantic thing you've ever said."

He smiled against the pillow. "Give it time. I've got edits."

Redrafting Love

The first thing Harper noticed about the book tour wasn't the crowds.

It was the silence in the hotel rooms.

After nearly a year of writing beside Elias—of coffee cups and overlapping laptops, of shared edits and quiet glances— the absence of *his* presence became its own character. She woke to silence. Fell asleep to email alerts. Ate room service alone. Signed hundreds of books without the weight of his hand at her back.

It wasn't loneliness.

Not quite.

Just... adjustment.

The kind you don't realize you need until it sits beside you in a king-sized hotel bed with no one to pass the pen to.

***

Her tour schedule stretched across eight weeks.

Boston. New York. Chicago. Denver. Seattle. L.A. Then London and Edinburgh.

The reviews were glowing.

Readers were warm.

Panels were thoughtful.

But none of it felt quite like *Ink & Embers* had. That book had felt like a heart cracked open and passed around.

This one?

It felt like her stepping forward alone—and trying not to flinch under the spotlight.

She called Elias after her third event.

He answered on the second ring.

"You look amazing," he said, without preamble. "I saw the panel. Someone shared a clip."

"I stammered."

"You breathed."

She smiled. "I miss you."

"I miss you more."

But the call only lasted ten minutes.

He had a submission due.

She had a podcast interview scheduled.

And before she could say *I love you*, the line clicked off.

***

Back at the cottage, Elias tried not to stare at the door every time the wind knocked a branch against it.

He filled the house with music.

With work.

With slow-cooked dinners he ended up eating alone.

But something else filled the space, too: opportunity.

One of his essays—*What I Didn't Say the First Time*—had been selected for a prestigious anthology.

Then, a week later, *The Paris Review* requested a personal submission for their winter issue.

And then, a TEDx curator emailed, asking if he would consider speaking at their next event.

The old Elias—the pre-Harper Elias—would have deleted the email.

But the man Harper had helped him become?

He left it open.

Unread.

Waiting.

Just like he was.

***

Two weeks later, Harper's tour brought her to Seattle, where she gave a keynote on "narrative bravery."

She talked about grief.

About silence.

About how the hardest part of telling your story isn't the telling—it's choosing who gets to hear it.

After the applause faded, she sat alone backstage, scrolling through her messages.

Still no response from her last text to Elias.

> *Thinking about you. About us.*
>
> *This feels like a weird dream I'm living without you in it.*

She stared at the words.

Then deleted them.

Then retyped them.

Then hit send.

Ten minutes later, her phone buzzed.

Elias:

> I feel the same. But maybe that means it's time we figure out how to live *with* each other in the dream, not just alongside it.

She exhaled.

Then smiled.

Then typed:

> So... does that mean you're coming to London?

His reply came almost instantly.

> Booked a flight an hour ago.

***

The hotel room in London was nothing like the cottage.

Harper had been upgraded to a boutique suite with large windows, soft lighting, and a complimentary bottle of wine chilling on the table.

But when Elias knocked on the door—jet-lagged, rumpled, and holding a paper bag from a café down the block—she realized she hadn't cared about the room at all until now.

"Hi," he said simply.

"Hi."

They didn't kiss.

Not right away.

Instead, they stood there for a second, like strangers who recognized each other in a dream and weren't sure if they could trust the memory.

Then Harper stepped forward and wrapped her arms around him.

He dropped the bag to the floor and held her tight.

Not like someone coming home.

Like someone trying to remember what home felt like.

***

They ordered takeout and sat cross-legged on the floor, sharing stories between bites of Indian curry and sips of wine.

Harper told him about the woman in Chicago who had asked if heartbreak could ever be a beginning.

Elias told her about the reader who had quoted his essay at a public reading without realizing the author was standing in the room.

"You're becoming famous," Harper teased.

He shrugged. "Famous to the people who need it. That's enough."

When the food was gone, they lay on the bed, side by side, hands brushing but not quite entwined.

Harper stared at the ceiling.

"It feels different," she whispered.

"What does?"

"Us."

Elias didn't reply right away.

Then: "We haven't had to share silence in a while."

She turned her head. "What if this new life doesn't leave room for silence?"

He reached for her hand. "Then we make room."

***

The next morning, Harper had a panel on "The Anatomy of Personal Narrative" at the British Library.

Elias insisted on coming.

He sat in the second row, listening as she spoke about storytelling as survival—how her first real story wasn't about love or loss, but about finally saying something she'd been afraid to for years: *"I don't want to be someone else's pen anymore."*

Afterward, readers lined up for signed copies.

Elias waited quietly by the back wall.

He watched her with a look somewhere between awe and sadness.

When she finally joined him, she could see it in his eyes.

"What is it?" she asked.

He paused. "You shine out here. But it feels like there's less room for me in the light."

Harper's chest tightened. "Elias—"

"I'm not asking you to dim," he said quickly. "I just don't know where I fit anymore."

She took his hand. "You're not the shadow, Elias. You're the reason I can stand in the light without fear."

He swallowed hard. "I want to believe that."

"Then let me prove it," she said.

He nodded.

But the doubt didn't vanish.

Not yet.

***

That night, they walked along the Thames, the city glittering in the dark water beside them.

"I've been offered a speaking slot," Elias said after a while. "At TEDx Cambridge."

Harper stopped. "What? When?"

"Next month."

Her face lit up. "That's incredible!"

He smiled faintly. "It is. But it scares me."

"Why?"

"Because if I say yes… it changes things."

"How?"

"I'm not the man in the cottage anymore."

Harper understood what he meant.

The recluse.

The mystery.

The safe distance.

"You're allowed to change," she said. "You're supposed to."

He looked at her, then whispered: "So are you."

***

Elias said yes to the TEDx talk.

Harper was the first person he called.

"You're going to be brilliant," she told him.

He didn't say thank you.

He just exhaled like a man who had been holding his breath since the first time someone asked him to speak his truth out loud.

The talk was scheduled for a Friday evening in Cambridge, at an intimate theatre with three hundred seats and minimal fanfare—just the way he preferred.

He called his talk:

The Story We Don't Publish: Grief, Silence, and Writing Our Way Back

The title alone made Harper's heart ache.

Not out of worry.

But because she knew how much it cost him to say those words into a room full of strangers.

She offered to help him prep.

But he declined.

"I have to find it on my own this time," he said.

***

Meanwhile, Harper returned to New York for a literary gala hosted by the National Book Foundation. She had been nominated in the "Debut Voice" category—a long shot, she thought.

So when her name was called that night, she stood too slowly and clapped for herself like it had happened to someone else.

She accepted the award with a brief, gracious speech.

She thanked Elias first.

"I would not be standing here," she said, "without the person who sat beside me in silence when I didn't yet know how to speak."

Backstage, she stared at the plaque like it belonged to another version of herself.

Not because she didn't earn it.

But because Elias wasn't there to hand her a crooked smile or a whispered *told you so*.

She called him afterward.

He answered, breathless, mid-draft.

"You did it," he said.

"We did it," she replied.

"No," Elias said gently. "You did this one alone. And that's what makes it matter."

***

In the days leading up to his TEDx talk, Elias shut himself away with index cards, voice notes, and the slow unraveling of memory.

He practiced in front of the mirror.

Recorded himself.

Deleted the recordings.

Started again.

It wasn't the content that scared him.

It was the exposure.

Once upon a time, grief had silenced him.

Now, the fear wasn't that people wouldn't listen.

It was that they *would*.

That they'd hear the cracks, the tremors, the unpolished truth.

The truth Harper had helped him excavate.

He scrolled back through her last text:

You taught me how to tell the truth and live with it.

He breathed.

And wrote the final line of his talk.

***

On the night of the event, Harper sat in the second row, fingers twisted in her lap.

Elias stepped onto the small, red circular carpet with no script in his hand—just a folded note in his pocket, his voice steady, his gaze fixed.

He began:

> "For a long time, I thought grief was something you buried.
>
> Then I realized it's something you build from."

He spoke for twelve minutes.

He didn't stammer.

He didn't falter.

And when he ended, it wasn't with applause in mind.

It was with one quiet sentence:

> "Sometimes the bravest thing we do is let someone read the pages we never meant to share."

The audience stood.

Harper stood with them.

And Elias looked directly at her.

That's when he smiled.

***

They celebrated over coffee and pastries in a small Cambridge café the next morning.

Harper held his hand across the table.

"You were magnificent," she said.

Elias blushed. "I was terrified."

"I couldn't tell."

"You could have been on that stage."

She shook her head. "That was yours. Completely."

He studied her. "It didn't feel like a version of us?"

"No," Harper said. "And that's what made it perfect."

There was a beat of quiet.

Then Elias asked, "Do you ever worry we're becoming… separate books?"

Harper tilted her head. "You mean, two different stories?"

He nodded.

"I think we've always been two stories," she said. "We just happened to share a chapter that changed us both."

Elias stared into his coffee.

"I don't want our next chapter to be an epilogue."

Harper reached for his hand again.

"Then let's write something new."

***

The idea came to Harper while re-reading Elias's TEDx transcript in a hotel bathtub, jet-lagged and wrapped in a towel with a notebook balanced on her knees.

Letters.

Not essays.

Not dialogue.

Letters.

Between them.

To each other.

No agenda. No revision. No filter.

Just the kind of truth they'd stopped saying out loud.

When she texted Elias the idea, his reply came quickly:

Let's call it: Ink Between Us.

Her heart skipped.

Deal.

***

They set rules.

One letter a week, for twelve weeks.

No discussion of the contents until all were written.

No editing.

No sending until the last one was finished.

Then, if they both agreed, they'd publish them. As-is.

Raw. Honest. Unafraid.

They didn't do it for readers.

They did it to find their way back through the fog.

To see who they were now—apart, together.

***

Harper's first letter began like this:

Dear Elias,

I miss writing next to you.

Not because I can't write without you. But because you made the silence feel like collaboration.

You never told me what to say. You just waited until I was brave enough to say it.

Elias's reply came days later, folded into a manila envelope left on her desk in the cottage.

Harper,

I always feared that the world would love your voice so much, it would forget we ever wrote together.

I didn't expect *you* to forget.

(I know you didn't mean to. But sometimes, silence feels like absence. And you've been quiet for a while.)

The letter stung.

Because it was true.

***

As the weeks passed, the letters deepened.

They weren't love notes.

They were explorations.

Admissions.

Some were poetic. Some clinical.

Some pages brimmed with longing.

Others held disappointment.

Harper: *You say you're proud, but I wonder if success makes you feel like I left you behind.*

Elias: *You say we're both growing, but I worry that I'm growing sideways while you're growing forward.*

They never read the letters together.

They wrote in different rooms, left the envelopes in a drawer between them.

By week six, the tension had changed.

Not angry.

Not accusatory.

But… honest.

Uncomfortably so.

***

One night, Harper sat alone at the table, reading over the letter she'd just written. It wasn't dramatic. No revelations. No confessions.

But it was real.

She ended it with:

> *I don't know if love can stretch this far.*
> *But if it breaks, I hope the pieces still spell your name.*

She folded it.

Slipped it into the envelope.

And wondered—for the first time—if truth might not bring them closer.

But draw the lines more clearly between who they were, and who they were becoming.

***

Elias's next letter didn't use her name until the final line. It began:

> *Sometimes I write to you and feel like I'm sending mail into another city. A beautiful one. But not mine anymore.*

And ended:

> *Still, I would rather write you from the border than stop writing altogether.*
> *Yours, still,*
> *Elias.*

***

At week ten, Harper nearly suggested stopping.
But she didn't.
Because something inside her believed that if they *could* finish this exchange—these twelve confessions, these layered truths—then they could find each other again.
Not in fiction.
Not in nostalgia.
But in the unflinching, complicated now.

***

The final letter sat in the drawer for three days before either of them touched it.

Twelve weeks.

Twelve envelopes.

Twelve truths that had cracked them open in quiet ways.

Neither of them had spoken about what the process had stirred up. Not out of avoidance. But out of reverence.

The drawer had become its own confessional.

And now, it was time to listen.

***

They made tea.

Not wine.

Not cocktails.

Just something warm and quiet to hold between them.

Elias brought the drawer to the table.

Laid the letters out like old photographs.

"You ready?" he asked.

Harper nodded.

They opened the first pair.

Then the second.

Then the third.

They didn't speak.

They just read.

One by one.

Side by side.

***

By letter five, Harper's throat had tightened.

By letter seven, Elias had stopped sipping his tea.

By letter nine, both had tears clinging to their lashes—but neither looked away.

Each letter peeled back a layer.

Some were fierce.

Some were frightened.

All were true.

> *I loved you more when you left the room sometimes. I finally saw myself without your shadow.*
>
> — Harper
>
> *I resented your success not because I wanted it, but because I didn't know who I was when I wasn't the broken one anymore.*
>
> — Elias
>
> *We mistook silence for intimacy. But sometimes silence is just fear wearing a velvet robe.*
>
> — Harper
>
> *I thought distance would show me who I am. But all it did was remind me who I only am when I'm with you.*
>
> — Elias

By the time they reached the final pair—Week 12—neither moved for a long moment.

"You first," Harper whispered.

Elias opened her letter with careful fingers.

Read in silence.

Then handed her his.

***

Elias's Final Letter:
Harper,
I don't know if love is a novel or a series of essays we keep revising with every version of ourselves.

But if this was our last page, I'd still choose the beginning a thousand times.

You taught me how to write again.

But more than that—you taught me how to live again.

If we never publish this, it will still be the most honest work I've ever done.

I don't need readers to witness it.

I just needed *you* to.

Yours—imperfect, in-process, still turning pages—
Elias

***

Harper's final letter was shorter than all the rest.
But every line pulsed with clarity.

Harper's Final Letter:
Elias,
We are not one book.

We are a shelf.

Of silence and fire.

Of grief and grit.

Of truth and trying again.

I will never stop reading you.
Even when the chapters get hard.
Even when they scare me.
I hope you'll keep reading me, too.
Love,
Harper

***

They sat in the silence that followed.
No one cried.
But no one smiled yet, either.
It wasn't resolution.
It was recognition.
That they were still learning how to hold each other while also holding their own pens.
That the story didn't have a clean ending.
That it *shouldn't*.

***

Finally, Elias reached for her hand.
Held it.
"Do we publish it?" he asked.
Harper looked at the stack of letters.
Then at him.
"No," she said. "Not yet."
He nodded. "But someday?"
She smiled. "Someday."

That night, they didn't talk much.

They didn't need to.

They cooked dinner together.

Read beside each other.

Laughed at something mundane.

Kissed in the hallway.

And when they went to bed, Harper reached across the pillow and said, "We're still us."

Elias kissed her palm.

"No matter how many drafts it takes."

***

Margins We Choose

The email came on a Thursday morning.

Subject: *Ink & Embers—Feature Film Interest*

Harper read it twice.

Then a third time.

Then slowly set down her tea and stared out the window, where Elias was in the garden, barefoot, reading.

She didn't interrupt him.

Not yet.

The email was from a senior acquisitions exec at LunaRiver Films—an independent studio known for prestige dramas with Oscar aspirations.

The kind of studio that adapted short story collections into masterpieces.

The kind that wanted intimacy, not explosions.

They weren't proposing an option.

They were offering a full deal—film rights, screenplay development, a director already attached.

The subject line had carried a quiet but undeniable subtext:

Let us retell what you lived.

***

She told Elias that evening, over dinner.

He didn't flinch.

Didn't ask for details.

Just looked at her carefully and said, "Do you want it?"

"I don't know," she admitted. "I thought I would. But now that it's here... I feel like they're trying to buy our *grief*."

"It *is* ours," he said.

She set down her fork. "What if they ruin it?"

Elias nodded. "What if they don't?"

That was the problem.

They could get it right.

Or wrong.

Or worse—almost right.

And in doing so, take a sacred, honest thing and turn it into something *almost meaningful*, but not *true*.

***

They agreed to take a meeting.

Just a conversation, they said.

A video call with the producers.

It lasted forty minutes.

The producer, Allison Ward, was thoughtful, articulate, and surprisingly well-read. She'd clearly studied the book. Quoted their lines back to them with reverence. Called their prose *"quietly devastating."*

Harper softened.

Until Allison said:

> "Of course, we'll need to open it up for screen. There's talk of setting the story in the Catskills instead of the coast, maybe introducing a flashback sequence of the fire itself... the kind of thing audiences respond to."

Elias froze.

Harper's smile faltered.

The producer continued.

"We want the essence. But we also want emotional *scale*. A little more action. A little more clarity around the romance arc."

"Clarity?" Elias asked, evenly.

"Well," Allison said with a laugh, "some viewers might not pick up on the nuance. We'd want to make it more explicit— when the characters fall in love, how it builds."

Elias said nothing.

Just scribbled something in the margin of the meeting notes.

Later, Harper would find it:

If you have to explain it, you've already missed it.

***

When the call ended, they sat in silence.

For once, not a comforting one.

Harper finally asked, "Would you be okay seeing someone play you?"

Elias shook his head. "It wouldn't be me. Not really."

"Maybe it's not supposed to be."

"That's the part that scares me."

Harper nodded.

She understood.

They had written the book to survive.

To reclaim the pieces they had both lost.

Turning that into entertainment felt like peeling the bark off a tree to paint it better colors.

***

The next day, Harper asked for the draft screenplay.

Just to read.

To understand.

To see how it might feel.

It arrived within a week.

One hundred and two pages.

Beautifully written.

Emotionally honest.

And wrong.

So wrong.

The fire was now a *scene*—vivid, slow-motion, scored to piano.

The first kiss was timed like a climax.

Their argument was a centerpiece.

Their reconciliation happened in a rainstorm, complete with declarations and sweeping camera pans.

It was everything audiences would love.

And nothing *they* had actually lived.

***

Harper read it first.

Elias read it second.

Neither spoke until after dinner.

They sat across from each other at the writing table.

Two copies of the script, marked up with highlighters and pencil notes.

Elias was the first to break the silence.

"Do you think it's bad?"

Harper sighed. "No. It's not bad."

"It's not ours."

She nodded.

"That's the problem," he said.

***

The next email from LunaRiver Films came with numbers.

Seven figures.

A six-month turnaround.

An A-list actress "interested in Harper's character."

Two production companies "willing to co-finance."

And a single line that rang louder than all the dollar signs combined:

> *We believe this story could become the next "literary phenomenon" to break into global film consciousness.*

Harper closed her laptop slowly.

It felt like staring at a list of ingredients for a beautiful meal—one that would be served to strangers who'd never know the names of the people who harvested the grain.

***

She found Elias outside, barefoot again, pulling weeds from the garden bed with more intensity than was necessary.

208

She didn't speak right away.

Just crouched beside him, brushing dirt from his wrist.

"They want to buy it," she said.

"I figured."

"They want to make it big."

"Let me guess," Elias said, not looking up. "More flashbacks. Maybe a climactic breakup followed by a rainy reunion."

She didn't laugh.

Neither did he.

"Do you feel like this is ours to say yes or no to?" she asked after a pause.

He looked at her.

"More than anything I've ever written," he said. "This story is ours."

***

The studio followed up with a call from the screenwriter himself—a thoughtful man named Carson who had clearly loved the book.

"I get it," Carson said. "You're afraid we'll take something sacred and turn it into a spectacle."

"Yes," Harper said bluntly.

"But that's not what we're after," he replied. "We want to honor the emotion. We want to put it into a different form."

"By rewriting it?" Elias asked.

"By translating it," Carson said.

But that was the problem.

Translation still required interpretation.

And interpretation, inevitably, meant change.

***

That night, Elias pulled *Ink & Embers* off the shelf and read it cover to cover.

Harper did the same.

They read separately, in different rooms.

When they met back at the kitchen table, the question hung in the air.

Not "should we?"

But can we live with it if we do?

"I'm afraid," Elias said.

Harper reached for his hand. "Of what?"

"That we'll watch it, someday, in a theater," he said quietly, "and wonder who those people are supposed to be."

Harper swallowed.

"Would you feel differently," she asked, "if we were the ones to write the screenplay?"

Elias blinked.

A beat passed.

Then another.

And then: "Maybe."

***

The next morning, Harper emailed the studio.

She didn't accept the offer.

She didn't reject it either.

She proposed something else.

We'd like to adapt the screenplay ourselves.
If this is going to live beyond the page, we want to be the ones to draw the lines.

The studio didn't respond immediately.
But two days later, a new reply came:

Unorthodox. Risky.
But your book was both of those things, too.
Let's talk.

***

It started the way it always had—with two mugs of coffee and a blank page.

But this time, the blank page wasn't a novel.

It was a screenplay.

Format. Structure. Scene headings. Dialogue clipped and technical. No room for long, lyrical paragraphs or inner monologue.

"It feels... skeletal," Elias muttered after their first few hours.

Harper glanced over her laptop. "That's the point. Film isn't the prose. It's the *spaces between*."

Elias stared at the blinking cursor.

"I liked the spaces between better when they were metaphors."

Harper laughed. "Yeah, well—this time we don't get to leave the camera in the room and hope it catches the silence."

**

They worked in short bursts.

Mornings for dialogue.

Afternoons for revision.

Evenings to read aloud what they'd written.

Some scenes flowed easily—like the one where Harper's fictional counterpart walks into the seaside cottage for the first time and finds the writer not typing, but staring out the window.

"She says, 'You're not what I expected,'" Harper read aloud.

Elias nodded. "And he says, 'Good. You'll be less disappointed when I fail you.'"

They both paused.

It hadn't been written that way in the book.

But it felt *truer* somehow—now that time had softened the memory.

**

Other scenes weren't so easy.

The fight.

The walkout.

The accusation that Harper had only returned to make Elias *publishable*.

Elias hovered over that scene in the draft for nearly an hour.

"Do we need it?" he asked.

Harper looked up. "It happened."

"Yes," he said. "But maybe not like that."

"Elias," she said gently, "this isn't just our story anymore. It's a story being told *through* us."

"I know," he said, quietly. "And that's what terrifies me."

***

For the first time in months, they disagreed on process.

Harper wanted to restructure the midpoint.

Elias wanted to keep the original sequence of events— messy, out of order, honest.

"Real life isn't a three-act structure," he argued.

"But film is," she replied. "We have to find *the version* of the truth that still feels like us—*and* works onscreen."

They went quiet.

Not in anger.

But in recognition of the tension between memory and meaning.

Finally, Elias said, "We're not just writing a story. We're writing *ourselves,* again."

"And we've changed," Harper said.

"Yes," Elias replied. "And I don't want to revise us into something more palatable."

She closed her laptop slowly.

"Then let's promise," she said. "We tell the truth—even if it's ugly. Even if it's quiet."

Elias met her eyes.

"Even if they cut it."

***

Midway through the second act, they hit a wall.

The fire.

It was the emotional core of the book—but in the screenplay, it felt sensationalized.

Every version the studio had suggested made it louder. Bigger. Cinematic.

But Elias didn't want to show the flames.

He wanted to show the *after*.

The stillness. The silence. The survivor's guilt.

"It's not the fire that shaped me," he said. "It's what I didn't say afterward."

Harper nodded.

"What if we don't show the fire at all?" she asked. "What if we only show him standing outside the wreckage, unable to go in?"

Elias looked at her.

"That," he said softly, "is the truest scene I can imagine."

***

They wrote it that way.

No flames.

Just a man.

Smoke.

The sound of waves behind him.

A choice he can't make.

A life already lost.

***

Weeks passed.

They found their rhythm again.

Not the old one.

Not quite.

This rhythm was quieter.

Wiser.

Less about proving themselves to each other—and more about protecting what they'd built.

Each scene became a negotiation.

Not of ego.

But of memory.

And by the time they reached the final page, it didn't feel like surrender.

It felt like ceremony.

***

Elias clicked save on the final draft.

Harper leaned back in her chair.

They looked at each other across the screen.

"We did it," she said.

He nodded.

"We told the truth. Again."

***

The studio's response came three days later.

A 12-page feedback memo.

It was cordial. Complimentary. Professional.

It was also clear:

"The script is emotionally rich but narratively sparse."

"We'd love to see more momentum in the second act."

"The final confrontation is too quiet."

"Consider a visual representation of the fire for emotional payoff."

"Audiences need more closure."

Harper stared at the screen, jaw clenched.

Elias read it standing up, pacing the writing room like a caged animal.

"They want closure," he said flatly.

"They want explosions," Harper muttered.

"They want a version of us that people can consume without discomfort."

Harper didn't argue.

Because he wasn't wrong.

***

That night, they opened a bottle of wine and read the memo again.

Line by line.

Note by note.

Harper highlighted the phrases that offered compromise: *"Consider"*, *"Would you be open to..."*, *"Alternative suggestions..."*

Elias crossed out anything that felt like dilution.

"I won't rewrite the silence," he said. "That moment after she walks out? It *has* to breathe."

"I know," Harper replied.

He looked at her. "But you also want this made."

She didn't deny it.

"I do. But not like *that*."

***

Two days later, they had a call with Allison Ward, the lead producer.

She was polite.

Even warm.

But underneath the cordial tone was clear pressure.

"You two have created something delicate. Beautiful. But this is film—we need arcs. Emotion needs amplification."

"What you call amplification," Elias said, "we call distortion."

"Elias," she replied gently, "this isn't a documentary. It's a *story*. We have to think about what resonates on screen."

Harper cut in. "We've written screenplays. This isn't about ignorance. It's about protection."

"We're offering you a chance to be involved," Allison said. "But that comes with collaboration."

"And what if we say no?" Elias asked.

A pause.

Then: "Then we'll need to move forward without you. You'll retain your story credit. But the screenplay will be reassigned."

***

After the call, Harper sat on the porch with a mug of cold tea, staring at the crashing waves.

Elias sat beside her, silent.

The wind tugged at her hair.

Finally, he spoke.

"I can't watch them rewrite it."

Harper didn't look at him. "I know."

"I won't be in the room when they do."

"I wouldn't ask you to."

A long silence.

Then Harper said, "But I might be."

That broke something in the air.

Elias turned toward her. "You're considering staying?"

"I'm considering... *guarding it*. From inside."

"You think you can?"

"I don't know. But if we leave, we lose all say. If I stay..."

"You become the last defense," he finished.

She nodded.

***

That night, Harper didn't sleep.

She reread the memo twice.

Not as a writer.

218

As a strategist.

A survivor.

She saw what they were trying to do—not destroy the story, but sand it smooth. Turn the jagged, personal edges into digestible beats.

They weren't villains.

Just... risk-averse.

And that, she realized, was the true danger.

The kind of editing that felt like polishing, but erased what made the thing *alive*.

She opened her laptop and wrote a new memo.

A counter-proposal.

Scene by scene.

Line by line.

What they'd keep.

What they'd *never* touch.

And what they might be willing to shape—slightly.

When she finished, she forwarded it to Elias.

Subject: *Only if we agree.*

His reply came before she could close the laptop.

If you're staying in the room,
I'll trust the fire to you.

***

The first thing Harper did was draw a line through the fire scene.

A literal line.

Thick and final.

Next to it, she wrote in block letters:

NO FLAMES. NO FLASHBACK.
MEMORY ONLY.

The second thing she did was circle the confrontation scene—the one where the characters fought, miscommunicated, unraveled.

THIS STAYS.
But let it be quiet. Let them talk like people, not screenplays.

The rest of her memo was a mixture of redlines, margin notes, and bold compromises.

One line she underlined three times:
Do not clarify their love story.
The ambiguity *is* the truth.

***

The studio called the revised memo "principled."
Allison called it "sharp."
Carson, the screenwriter, called it "refreshingly defiant."
But none of them said no.
In fact, they said yes.
With a few adjustments.
One compromise on pacing.
One scene slightly restructured.
But the heart?

Intact.

The ending?

Unchanged.

The silence?

Preserved.

***

When Harper hung up, she sat on the cottage porch and called Elias.

He answered with a cautious, "Well?"

"I kept the fire out," she said.

"And the kiss in?"

"Unscripted. Just a breath between them. A maybe."

Elias let out a long, quiet sigh.

"Thank you."

"For what?"

"For protecting the version of us I can still live with."

Harper stared at the sea. "I did it for both of us."

"I know," he said. "And I never doubted that you could."

***

The following month was a whirlwind.

Contracts.

Legal language.

Production timelines.

But Harper kept her seat at the table—not just as writer, but as executive producer.

Elias declined all official titles.

But one night, over wine and script pages, he handed her a small envelope.

Inside was a card that read:

> To *the woman who kept the pen steady when the rest of the world offered erasers.*

She didn't cry.
But she closed her eyes and memorized it.
Word for word.
Like a vow.

***

When filming began, Harper flew to the set in Nova Scotia—chosen for its rocky coastline, its wind-whipped silence, its lighthouse.

Elias didn't go.

He stayed home, worked on poems, taught a few workshops.

But every night, he called her.

And every night, she described it all:

The quiet click of the clapperboard.

The actress who had read the book five times and cried before her first take.

The director who shot the silent beach scene in one, trembling, perfect take.

It wasn't their story exactly.

But it wasn't anyone else's either.

It was something in between.

And maybe that was the point.

Two months later, Harper returned to the cottage.

Tired. Fulfilled. Weather-worn.

She found Elias in the kitchen, making tea.

He looked up, saw her, and smiled like nothing had ever changed.

"Did they get it right?" he asked.

She stepped forward and wrapped her arms around him.

"No," she whispered. "But they didn't get it wrong."

***

That night, they curled up on the sofa and read their favorite lines from the shooting script.

Not the polished version.

The *real* one.

The one with their fingerprints in the margins.

The one where love didn't need narration.

Just a pause.

A look.

A held breath.

***

As they turned off the lights, Harper whispered into the dark:

"Do you ever wish we'd said no?"

Elias was quiet for a moment.

Then: "Sometimes."

Harper smiled sadly.

"Me too."

"But only for a second," he added. "Then I remember the real ending."

She turned toward him.

"What ending?"

He kissed her temple and said,

"The one where we let the world in…
but didn't let it rewrite us."

***

The Quiet Between Applause

The first time Harper saw *Ink & Embers* on the big screen, she held her breath.

Not because she was nervous.

But because, for the first time, she wasn't watching a performance.

She was watching a memory translated into motion.

The premiere was small and private—an early screening at a film festival in the Berkshires.

Elias didn't go.

He had said gently, "You'll tell me if it's ours."

So Harper sat alone in the back row, her name listed in the credits, her heart thudding like a second pulse.

When the lights dimmed and the screen flickered to life, the quiet hit first.

Not a score.

Not a voiceover.

Just wind and waves and an empty cottage on a gray coast.

She smiled.

They had listened.

***

The film wasn't perfect.

But it was patient.

Where the book had offered language, the film offered silence.

Where the letters had confessed, the camera lingered.

There was a scene—one Harper hadn't written, but had allowed—where the woman stands alone in the cottage, reading a letter by candlelight. She doesn't cry. She doesn't speak.

She just breathes.

And somehow, it felt like all the stories they hadn't written down were contained in that single breath.

When the credits rolled, the applause was soft.

Then rising.

Sustained.

Harper didn't clap.

She just exhaled.

***

Two days later, the reviews started pouring in.

Variety called the film "a quietly devastating portrait of creative intimacy."

The New Yorker praised it as "the rare adaptation that doesn't try to improve the book—it just listens to it."

IndieWire wrote: *"This is the kind of love story we don't see enough—one built on stillness, compromise, and respect."*

Harper forwarded that one to Elias.

His reply came within minutes.

They saw us.

***

Then came the interviews.

The press junkets.

The morning shows that wanted the "real-life love story" behind the film.

The problem?

No one could agree on what that story *was*.

Some headlines speculated that Harper had written the book as a way to "save" Elias.

Others suggested Elias had "manipulated" the narrative to gain sympathy.

A few praised the book as a radical feminist take on creative identity.

Others called it "emotional co-dependence in literary clothing."

They were all wrong.

And, somehow, a little bit right.

***

Harper did a few interviews.

She stuck to the script.

"It's a story about finding your voice after losing everything."

"It's fiction. But we wrote from truth."

"It's not about one person saving another. It's about two people learning how to stop hiding."

Elias refused all interview requests.

Even when the studio begged.

Even when Harper gently asked.

"I've already told my part," he said. "In the book. And the letters. Everything else is noise."

One evening, after back-to-back interviews in New York, Harper called Elias from her hotel suite.

"They keep asking how we fell in love."

"What do you say?"

"I say… we didn't fall. We unfolded."

Elias chuckled softly on the other end. "I like that."

"But I don't think they get it."

"They're not supposed to."

"I know," she whispered. "But I wish they'd stop trying to explain us."

There was a pause.

Then Elias said, "Let them talk. Let them guess. The ones who need the real story will find it."

***

The studio pushed for a wider release.

More press.

More appearances.

A magazine wanted a full photo spread of Harper and Elias "in the cottage where the story began."

They declined.

Politely.

Firmly.

Because some places didn't belong to stories.

Some places were still home.

***

And yet, the world kept reaching.

Readers flooded Harper's inbox with questions.

Some heartfelt.

Some invasive.

> *Did the fire really happen?*
>
> *Is Elias real?*
>
> *Was the argument in the book the one that nearly broke you?*

The worst one?

> *Do you still love him?*

She never replied.

Not because she didn't know the answer.

But because the answer wasn't a sound bite.

It was a choice.

Made every day.

In silence.

In space.

In letters and shared cups of coffee and in letting each other breathe without always being asked to perform.

***

It was a gray Wednesday morning when Elias published the op-ed.

No announcement.

No promotion.

Just a quiet link that appeared in *The Atlantic*, tucked under the Culture section:

"Let Me Be the Quiet One: On Love, Legacy, and the Cost of Telling Your Own Story"

It was 2,400 words.
Measured.
Precise.
Not a defense.
Not a rebuttal.
Just... truth.

***

In the opening paragraph, Elias wrote:

> *I am not a character. I am not a metaphor.*
> *I am a man who lived through grief, found voice in partnership,*
> *and wrote something true beside someone braver than I was.*
> *But let's be clear: our book is not a confession. It is not a*
> *product. It is not an invitation to decode our love like a riddle.*

The piece was beautiful.
But it was also firm.
When you ask, 'Did she save you?' you strip us both of agency.
When you say, 'You must be the muse,' you miss the point entirely.
We didn't write a romance. We wrote a reckoning.
And we are still writing it—daily. Privately. Deliberately.

***

Harper read it in the kitchen, tears sliding down her cheeks before she realized she was crying.

It wasn't the eloquence.

It was the *freedom*.

The way Elias gave her space, even in his own voice.

He hadn't named her.

He hadn't needed to.

He had given her the dignity of not being explained.

***

The piece went viral.

Within hours, it was trending across Twitter and literary blogs.

Think pieces emerged within the day:

> *"The Rise of the Anti-Muse: Why Women Don't Need to Inspire to Create."*
> *"Emotional Labor in Literature: What Elias Hale Gets Right."*
> *"Private Love, Public Story: When Authors Draw the Line."*

Some praised his clarity.

Others called it calculated.

One journalist accused him of "weaponized modesty."

Elias didn't respond to any of it.

Neither did Harper.

They didn't need to.

***

Still, the ripple effects came.

More requests.

TV segments.

Panel invitations.

A streaming service offered them a six-part docuseries about the "real-life couple behind *Ink & Embers.*"

They declined.

Again.

But the weight of being watched began to press down.

Elias could feel it in the way strangers lingered at his poetry readings now, asking questions that had nothing to do with the poems.

Harper felt it in bookstores, where readers whispered as she passed, as if trying to match her face to the woman onscreen.

The quiet they had once fought for was becoming harder to hold.

***

One night, after a long dinner, Harper looked across the table and asked, "Do you think we made a mistake letting it all be seen?"

Elias was quiet.

Then: "No."

"But?"

"But I think we forgot that being heard comes with echoes."

Harper rubbed her temples. "I'm tired of being interpreted."

Elias reached for her hand. "Then stop explaining."

"I try. But people keep asking the same thing."

"Let them ask."

"And say nothing?"

"No," Elias said. "Say something else. Say what only you can."

***

The next morning, Harper sat down at her desk and wrote a short essay of her own.

Just 800 words.

A refusal disguised as reflection.

She titled it:

What I Won't Say About Us.

***

She published it on her own blog. No media blitz. No fanfare.

It read, in part:

> This is not a clarification. This is not a backstory.
>
> I am not here to tell you how we met, what we felt, or when we knew.
>
> I am only here to remind you that stories—even true ones—are not blueprints.
>
> They are doors.
>
> You may walk through.
>
> But you do not get to rearrange the furniture.

She closed the piece with a simple note:

> Some things we write for ourselves.
>
> And some things, we never write at all.

The wind had returned to the coast.

That brisk, salt-laced kind that whipped hair into eyes and reminded you that nature didn't care about critical acclaim or comment sections.

Harper stood at the edge of the property, toes pressed to the cold wooden slats of the deck, watching the tide roll in like punctuation.

A full stop.

A breath.

A pause they'd long needed.

Elias stepped out behind her, a mug of tea in each hand.

She took hers without speaking.

They didn't need to say it aloud: They were retreating. Not running. Not hiding.

Just… retreating.

The difference mattered.

***

They stayed offline.

Turned off news alerts.

Unsubscribed from Google notifications.

No interviews. No readings. No social media.

Just groceries, long walks, books they never finished, and conversations that didn't need to be profound.

They cleaned out the storage shed.

Fixed the rusted hinges on the cottage's back door.

Planted new lavender in the garden, even though they both admitted they'd probably forget to water it.

They slept in.

Cooked together.

Read to each other.

Laughed when the wind knocked over the patio chairs for the third time in a week.

The stillness returned like an old friend.

One they hadn't realized they missed.

***

One morning, Elias found Harper at the dining table, sketching on a napkin with a pen that barely worked.

"What's that?" he asked, pouring coffee.

"Just a scene," she said.

"For a book?"

She shrugged. "Maybe. Or maybe just for me."

Elias smiled. "The best ones start that way."

She looked at him. "Do you ever want to write another book together?"

He considered.

"Not now," he said.

"Because of everything?"

"No," he replied. "Because we already told the one we needed to tell. Anything else would be *about* us, not *for* us."

Harper nodded.

That made sense.

***

They took to walking every evening just before dusk.

No phones.

No agenda.

Just their boots crunching against the damp earth and the sea roaring its indifference a few yards away.

Sometimes they talked.

Sometimes they didn't.

Once, Harper asked, "What would we have done if *Ink & Embers* had failed?"

Elias stopped walking.

"I think we still would've found each other," he said.

"You do?"

"Yes. But maybe slower. Maybe quieter."

Harper smiled. "Maybe better."

He offered his arm. "Or maybe worse."

She laughed. "But still."

"Still," he agreed.

And they kept walking.

***

At night, they reread old books aloud.

Not theirs.

Never theirs.

They read Neruda, Didion, Baldwin, and Bishop.

They made up voices for characters.

Disagreed on themes.

Argued over comma placements like it mattered.

Because in a world obsessed with publishing, releasing, and responding, they'd found peace in not producing anything at all.

***

One evening, Harper reached into the drawer where they'd stored the twelve letters—the ones they'd written to each other during their hardest season.

She placed them on the table.

Elias raised an eyebrow.

"What are you thinking?" he asked.

She shrugged.

"Nothing," she said. "I just wanted to remember."

He picked one up—Week 7, he noted—and read the line where Harper had written:

If we break, I hope the pieces still spell your name.

Elias closed the envelope and said, "We didn't break."

"No," Harper said. "But we cracked."

He reached across the table and touched her wrist.

"And we let the light in."

***

The invitation came in the form of a handwritten letter.

Elegant stationery. Ink that bled slightly at the edges.

It was from the Hawthorne Bay Residency, a quiet literary retreat nestled in a small town on the coast of Maine.

We admire not only your work but the generosity behind it, the letter read.

We would be honored if you would serve as our dual Writers-in-Residence for the coming season.

One month. Eight emerging writers. One shared story space.

Harper turned the envelope over in her hands twice before showing it to Elias.

He read it slowly.

Then looked at her with a small smile.

"We'd be the mentors now."

She nodded. "Are we old enough for that?"

He chuckled. "Emotionally? Definitely. Physically? I still get carded at wine bars."

She laughed. But her fingers tightened slightly around the paper.

"You want to do it?" Elias asked.

"I think so," she said. "But only if you do."

He nodded.

Then said what they were both thinking:

"Teaching our story is one thing.

Letting others write into it… that's something else entirely."

***

They arrived at Hawthorne Bay in late spring.

The coast there was softer than their own—less jagged, more pine and fog than salt and rock.

The retreat house was a refurbished Victorian cottage with ten bedrooms, two common areas, and floor-to-ceiling windows that filled the rooms with light.

The other writers were already there when they arrived.

Twenty-somethings and thirty-somethings, wide-eyed, wildly talented, all of them carrying notepads, headphones, or pens like lifelines.

They knew who Harper and Elias were.

Some tried not to show it.

Others didn't bother hiding it.

One, a red-haired poet named Mara, whispered over dinner, "*Ink & Embers* is the reason I started writing again after my divorce."

Harper thanked her softly.

But the compliment sat heavy on her chest.

Praise was no longer applause.

It was pressure.

***

The first few days were gentle.

Morning workshops. Afternoon writing blocks. Evening readings.

Harper led a session on narrative tension.

Elias taught a class called "Writing Without a Mask."

They worked well together—finishing each other's sentences, tossing teaching duties back and forth with ease.

But after a few days, the intimacy of the space began to reveal something else:

Their story had become myth.

A young man named James asked during Q&A, "How did you know you were each other's *ending*?"

Elias blinked.

Harper hesitated.

Then answered, "We didn't."

"But you are, right?" someone added. "The ending?"

Elias looked at Harper.

And said, honestly: "We're still writing."

***

Later that night, Harper sat at the edge of the dock overlooking the bay.

Elias joined her with two mugs of cocoa and a silence that said he already knew what was on her mind.

"They want the fairytale," Harper murmured.

"I don't blame them."

"No," she agreed. "But it's strange."

"What is?"

"To realize we're a mirror people are using to check their own reflection."

Elias sipped his drink.

"They don't want our story," he said. "They want *permission* to believe theirs might end well too."

***

During week two, something shifted.

One of the residents, a novelist named Camille, handed Elias her manuscript-in-progress and said:

> *'It's a romance, but messy. I used a lot of what you said in the 'Writing Without a Mask' class.'*

Elias read it overnight.
It was brilliant. Tender. Bold.
The ending was unresolved—intentionally so.
The characters part ways.
No kiss.
No promise.
Just a long look across a quiet room.
Camille's note at the end read:

> I think love is letting someone go and still hoping they'll turn back around.

> Thank you for reminding me that's still a love story.

Elias showed it to Harper.
She smiled.
Then, for the first time in months, said:
"I think I'm ready to write something new."

***

They left the residency under a soft gray sky, with the smell of pine in their clothes and ink stains on their hands.

The farewell dinner had been understated. No speeches. No tearful goodbyes. Just shared food, laughter, and one simple toast from Mara, the poet:

"To stories that never end,

and the people brave enough to live them out loud."

Harper had blinked back tears.

Elias had squeezed her hand beneath the table.

They didn't say much as they packed.

Just folded clothes. Collected their notebooks. Left a small bundle of their favorite used books behind in the reading room, with a note on the top:

Some stories are written alone.

But the best ones are read together.

***

Back at the cottage, everything felt smaller.

Quieter.

Not in a bad way.

More like returning to a song you'd once loved and finding a new note buried in the melody.

Harper stood in the doorway of the kitchen for a long moment.

"Smells like home again," she said.

Elias, already unpacking a bag of tea, glanced up and smiled. "That's because I cleaned the fridge."

She laughed. "Miracle worker."

"Poet first. Miracle worker second."

She stepped over and kissed his cheek.

"Both," she said. "Always both."

***

They spent the next few days in soft rhythms.

Groceries.

Emails.

A new shelf for the growing pile of books gifted to them by residents who had signed the inside covers with things like:

Thank you for reminding me that my voice is enough.

You gave me permission to finish what I was afraid to start.

Harper ran her fingers over those inscriptions one night and whispered, "Maybe legacy isn't about being remembered."

Elias looked up from his chair. "What is it, then?"

"About helping someone else remember themselves."

***

They didn't plan to write again so soon.

But on the fifth night back, Harper woke up at 2:17 a.m. with a sentence fully formed in her mind.

She scribbled it on the back of a receipt and placed it on the writing table.

When Elias came in the next morning, he read it and smiled:

Love isn't the plot. It's the margin where the reader writes their own notes.

He tapped his fingers thoughtfully.

Then added underneath:

And sometimes, that margin is the best part of the story.

***

A week later, they agreed to start again.

Not a sequel.

Not a confession.

Not a "what happened after."

Something new.

A novel.

Loosely inspired by the retreat.

By the echoes.

By the way love can be present even when it's not spoken.

Elias called it: "a story with the lights turned down."

Harper called it: "a love story no one would recognize… except the people who needed it."

They wrote slowly.

Gently.

Without deadline.

Without pressure.

Just two people, at the table where it had all begun, finding a new voice.

Together.

***

They didn't talk about reviews anymore.

Or film rights.

Or what the public thought they should do next.

Instead, they went for walks.

Tried new recipes.

Read scenes aloud and scratched them out just for the pleasure of disagreeing.

Sometimes Harper would read one of Elias's old poems and say, "You were always writing us. Even when I hadn't arrived yet."

And sometimes Elias would find Harper's notes in the margins of her old drafts—little comments like:

"Too tender. Leave it in anyway."

And he'd smile, thinking:

Still tender. Still here.

***

One evening, they lit a fire outside, wrapped themselves in mismatched blankets, and sat watching the flames dance quietly between them.

Elias looked over.

"Do you miss it?"

Harper raised an eyebrow. "The chaos?"

"No. The applause."

She thought for a moment.

Then: "I used to think that was the prize. Being seen. Heard. Applauded."

"And now?"

She reached for his hand.

"I think this is the prize," she said. "Getting to live the story after the last page."

They didn't know what the next chapter would be.

But they didn't need to.

For now, the story was simple.

And enough.

***

Where the Story Waits

The call came just before breakfast.

Harper answered out of habit—still half-dreaming, barefoot, a tea towel in her hand.

It was Mara, the red-haired poet from the residency.

Her voice was thinner than Harper remembered.

Shaky.

"I didn't know who else to call," she said. "Camille died last night."

Harper blinked.

Felt the world tilt.

"What?"

"She—she was in a car accident. She was hit crossing the street. The driver didn't see her."

Silence.

"I'm so sorry," Harper whispered. "Elias and I... we loved her. We both did."

"I know," Mara said, voice cracking. "I thought... you should know."

***

Harper didn't speak for a long time after the call.

She stood in the kitchen, unmoving.

Elias found her there, unmoving, holding the tea towel in her hand like it was still warm.

He touched her back gently.

"She's gone," Harper said, the words dull. "Camille."

Elias didn't ask how.

Didn't say *What?*

He simply pulled her in and held her against his chest until the weight began to find shape.

***

Camille.

The brilliant young writer who had handed them a manuscript about unresolved love.

The one who had said, *"Thank you for reminding me that an unfinished story is still worthy."*

The one who had helped Harper remember that creating wasn't just about healing—it was about hope.

Gone.

***

That night, they didn't write.

Didn't read.

Just sat on the floor in front of the unlit fireplace, knees touching, silent.

"I keep hearing her voice," Harper murmured.

"Me too," Elias said.

Harper looked at him.

"She wasn't done."

"No," Elias agreed. "But she gave so much while she was here."

Harper nodded.

"But I can't stop thinking... if we hadn't taken that residency. If we hadn't said yes. Would I even have known her?"

Elias looked at her gently.

"And if we hadn't—she might not have written that book."

247

***

The next morning, Harper pulled Camille's manuscript from the shelf where it had been tucked away for safekeeping.

The title: *The Unsaid Season*

A story of two women who never confessed what they felt, but lived in the quiet ache of almost.

Harper ran her fingers over the pages.

She hadn't read it in full since the residency.

Now, each word hummed with new weight.

Elias sat beside her and said, "We should help finish it."

Harper looked at him. "But it was already finished."

"I know," he said. "But it's not *out* there. We could help her parents publish it. Maybe even write a foreword."

She swallowed. "I don't want to edit it."

"We won't," Elias promised. "We'll protect it. Like someone once did for us."

***

Over the next few days, they reached out to Mara, who connected them with Camille's sister.

There were tears.

Emails.

An exchange of handwritten notes and permission.

Camille's family had known about the manuscript but didn't know what to do with it.

They gave Harper and Elias their blessing.

"Do what you think she would have wanted," her sister said.

248

So they did.

***

They didn't rush.
Didn't reframe.
Just compiled it—exactly as Camille left it.
Raw.
Beautiful.
Unresolved.
Harper wrote the foreword.
Elias proofread it.
Together, they made sure Camille's name reached the places she'd dreamed of.

***

In the weeks that followed, grief became a quiet guest in their home.
It didn't speak loudly.
Didn't sob or shatter.
It just… sat beside them.
Reminded them that even the best stories couldn't undo loss.
But they *could* carry it.
They could say: I was here.
I wrote.
I mattered.

***

The reading was held at a small bookstore in Portland—Camille's favorite.

Mismatched chairs.

Twinkling lights.

A chalkboard wall with poetry fragments written in colorful scrawl.

Mara had organized everything with care.

No cameras.

No press.

Just Camille's friends, her family, a handful of writers she'd admired, and readers who had discovered her manuscript in its early release and were already quoting it online.

The copies of *The Unsaid Season* sat on a single shelf near the back—softcover, simple design, no author photo.

Just Camille's name in elegant serif across the cover.

Harper ran her fingers over the stack when she arrived.

It didn't feel triumphant.

It felt sacred.

***

They each read a passage.

Mara went first—a poem Camille had written in a margin, never published.

Then Harper, reading from Camille's final chapter.

The line she chose echoed long after she closed the book:

"Love wasn't the ache.

It was the permission to feel it without apology."

When Harper sat down, Elias stood and read his foreword—his voice low, reverent.

"There are stories that shout.

Camille wrote one that *listened.*

May we all be brave enough to tell what we know, and gentle enough to leave the ending unfinished."

***

After the event, people stayed.

They shared stories.

Offered hugs.

Tears.

One woman whispered to Harper, "I thought I was the only one who felt that kind of love."

"You're not," Harper replied softly. "And you never were."

***

That night, back in their hotel room, Harper sat by the window, watching headlights blur across the wet street.

Elias had fallen asleep with a book on his chest.

She glanced at her notebook—closed, unused for days.

And then, slowly, she opened it.

At first, she just wrote Camille's name.

Then a few words beneath it:

> *You didn't get to finish your story.*
> *But you helped me start mine.*

She paused.

Then flipped to a new page.

And began.

Not about Elias.

Not about loss.

Not even about love.

Something else entirely.

A woman.

Alone.

On a beach.

Finding something buried in the sand.

Harper didn't know where it was going.

She just knew she needed to write it.

***

The next morning, she showed Elias the first page.

He read it in silence, then looked up with a raised brow.

"You're writing again."

"Feels strange."

"Feels *right*," he said.

She exhaled. "It's not about us."

"It doesn't have to be."

"I don't even know what it is."

Elias smiled and passed her a mug of coffee.

"Then keep going.

That's how all good stories start."

***

Back at the cottage, the rhythm changed again.

Not dramatically.

Just slightly.

Harper wrote in the mornings.

Elias gardened in silence.

They shared pages sometimes.

Critiqued less.

Encouraged more.

And sometimes, Harper would stop halfway through a sentence and whisper:

"Camille would have liked this character."

Elias would nod. "She's in there, you know. Somewhere in the lines."

Harper smiled.

"She's *between* the lines."

***

It started with silence.

Not the heavy kind that signaled tension.

Not the aching kind they'd once filled with letters and unfinished thoughts.

This silence was soft.

Productive.

Intentional.

Harper took the spare bedroom and turned it into a writing den.

Not for memoirs.

Not for love stories.

For something new.

A woman who wasn't her.

A life that wasn't familiar.

She lit a candle before writing.

Played cello music from a forgotten playlist.

And didn't let herself think about plot or purpose.

Just... rhythm.

Voice.
Breath.

***

Elias didn't ask questions.
Didn't peek over her shoulder.
Instead, he quietly returned to his old journals.
Pages he hadn't opened since before the book.
He began sifting through poems he'd written long ago, in margins and spiral notebooks, on napkins and envelope backs.
Some about Harper.
Some about fire.
Many about silence.
And more recently, poems about Camille.
About absence.
About what it meant to carry someone else's story forward without editing it to fit your own.

***

They worked for hours each day.
Rarely together.
But the cottage was small, and their proximity always comforted.
Harper would hear Elias tapping on the typewriter in the study.
Elias would hear Harper pacing, muttering dialogue, or laughing quietly to herself.
They rarely interrupted.

But at the end of each evening, they found each other in the kitchen.

Two bowls.

Two spoons.

Soup or pasta or simple roasted vegetables.

And, always, tea.

Harper would ask, "Good writing day?"

Elias would nod, or sometimes shrug and say, "Words showed up. That's enough."

Then they'd clink mugs and say:

"To the words that waited."

***

After two weeks, Elias began to assemble the poems into a small collection.

He didn't have a title yet.

But he started grouping them thematically—grief, quiet love, unfinished stories.

He wrote one poem that Harper found tucked inside a book on the coffee table:

There are people who teach you how to leave.

And then there are people who teach you how to stay.

You were neither.

You just taught me how to listen,

Even after the door closed.

Harper knew it was for Camille.

But she also knew it was for all of them.

***

She, too, was making progress.

Slow.

Unrushed.

The woman on the beach had turned into a coastal archeologist, unearthing things people thought were lost to time: messages in bottles, abandoned photographs, even pieces of old shipwrecks.

Harper didn't know where the story was going.

But she didn't care.

For the first time in years, she wasn't writing to fix anything.

Or to save herself.

She was just... exploring.

Uncovering.

Listening to a voice that wasn't her own, but still felt familiar.

Like echo.

Like memory.

Like instinct.

***

One night, Harper walked into the living room where Elias was reading.

She handed him a stack of ten pages.

He set the book down and looked at her.

"You sure?"

"No," she said. "But I want you to see it."

He read slowly.

Without expression.

Without annotation.

When he finished, he handed the pages back and said, "This doesn't sound like you."

Harper raised an eyebrow.

"No, I mean that in the best way," he clarified. "It's *free*."

She blinked.

Then smiled.

"Thank you."

"Keep going," Elias said, voice soft. "She's becoming someone I want to know."

***

The doubt didn't arrive all at once.

It crept in.

On the third week, Harper sat staring at her laptop for almost forty minutes before realizing she'd typed the same sentence five times—and deleted it each time.

It wasn't bad.

It just felt *pointless*.

She got up. Poured another cup of tea. Sat back down. Tried again.

Typed a new line.

Deleted it again.

Finally, she shut the lid.

Sat in silence.

And whispered, "What if this story doesn't matter?"

***

Later that evening, she mentioned it to Elias.

He was slicing carrots in the kitchen, sunlight warming his shoulders.

"What do you mean?" he asked.

She leaned on the counter, arms crossed. "I mean… what if it's just a nice idea? Just a woman and a beach and some introspection? What if no one cares?"

Elias didn't answer right away.

He dropped the carrots into the pot. Stirred. Then said, "Do you?"

"Do I what?"

"Do you care?"

She blinked. "Well, yes, obviously—"

"Then someone cares," he said gently. "And that's enough for now."

She gave a weak smile. "You always know how to say something that feels like an ending."

"It's a gift," he said, deadpan. "But not always helpful in soup-making."

***

The next day, Elias received an email.

It was from *Juniper & Co.*, a small but respected indie press.

They'd seen one of his newer poems in a literary journal and asked if he had more.

He did.

In fact, he had an entire collection.

He hesitated before responding.

The poems were raw.

Unfiltered.

They weren't about Harper—not directly—but she was in them.

So was Camille.

So was the version of himself he'd been before the fire.

So was the version who thought he'd never write again.

***

That night, he sat down beside Harper on the porch.

Told her about the offer.

"They want to see the manuscript."

Her eyes widened. "Elias, that's incredible."

"I'm not sure."

She tilted her head. "Why not?"

"They're not clean poems," he said. "They're unfinished. Messy. Honest."

"You think that makes them unworthy?"

"I think it makes them vulnerable."

Harper rested her hand on his knee.

"I think that makes them *necessary*."

***

Still, Elias waited three more days before sending the manuscript.

He titled it: *The Almosts and the After.*

No subtitle.

No explanation.

Just a dedication:

For the ones who left,
and the ones who stayed to listen.

***

Meanwhile, Harper returned to her own manuscript.

The fear was still there.

But something had shifted.

The pressure to impress was slowly unraveling, like a thread no longer needed to hold the fabric together.

She returned to the sentence she'd written—and deleted—five times.

And this time, she kept it.

> *Some things you don't bury to forget.*
> *You bury them so you can stop guarding the grave.*

***

The story began to grow.

The archeologist on the beach found a journal buried beneath a rotting ship plank.

Inside were fragments of a life never fully lived.

Not a love story.

Not a tragedy.

Just… evidence.

Of presence.

Of an attempt to speak.

Harper realized she wasn't writing a plot.

She was writing a quiet record.

A human echo.

And maybe that was enough.

***

The email arrived at 6:42 a.m.

Harper was still asleep, curled on her side, one hand pressed beneath the pillow, the other reaching instinctively toward the empty space where Elias had been moments before.

He stood barefoot in the kitchen, reading the words over and over:

> Dear Elias,
>
> We're honored to publish your manuscript.
>
> Your voice is quiet but profound. We believe this collection will find the readers who need it most.
>
> Let's begin.

There was no marketing plan.

No talk of film rights.

No publicist offering to "shape the narrative."

Just a simple yes.

And in that simplicity, Elias felt something uncoil in his chest.

Not pride.

Not excitement.

Something deeper.

Like return.

Like arrival.

***

He printed the email, placed it on the counter beside Harper's favorite mug, and began making coffee.

When she stumbled in, hair tousled and half-awake, she blinked at the paper.

Then read it.

Then looked up at him.

Her smile was slow. Warm. Wordless.

She crossed the room, wrapped her arms around him, and buried her face in his shoulder.

"You did it," she whispered.

He shook his head.

"We did," he said. "Even apart, we still write toward each other."

***

The next few weeks passed gently.

Elias worked with the editor from *Juniper & Co.*, making small changes to the manuscript. Nothing major. Just line-level clarity and spacing.

He insisted on keeping the rough edges.

The poems about Camille stayed in.

So did the one about Harper that simply read:

> You didn't ask me to stay.
>
> You just made the leaving unthinkable.

Harper continued writing her novel—more steadily now.

The woman on the beach had become a vessel for stories lost to time. Not a savior. Not a seeker. Just someone willing to sit still long enough to hear what others had forgotten how to say.

It wasn't a bestseller.

Not yet.

It wasn't even finished.

But it *was* hers.

Entirely.

***

One afternoon, Harper walked into the study and found Elias staring at an empty notebook.

"Writer's block?" she asked gently.

"Not exactly."

He turned the notebook toward her.

On the first page, he'd written a dedication:

> *To the ones who listen before they speak.*

She ran her fingers along the words.

Then looked at him.

"You're starting something new?"

He nodded. "I think I might have one more book in me."

She smiled. "I think you have many."

He smirked. "Flattery gets you nowhere."

"It gets me coffee," she said, already walking to the kitchen.

"Fair," he called after her. "Double shot, if you believe in me *that* much."

***

That evening, they sat on the porch with their notebooks open, the sky blushing lavender, the waves soft in the distance.

Neither spoke for a long time.

Then Harper asked, "Do you think it'll ever feel like it did… at the start?"

Elias thought for a moment.

263

"No," he said. "But I don't want it to."

She looked at him.

He continued, "Back then, we were writing to survive. Now, we're writing to stay."

***

As the sun dropped behind the horizon, Harper reached for Elias's hand.

No big speech.

No dramatic vow.

Just fingers entwined, hearts steady, pens resting on the pages of new stories they weren't afraid to begin.

***

Of Quiet Things and Promises

The first copy of *The Almosts and the After* arrived in a slim cardboard box.

No fanfare.

Just a soft thud at the door and a plain envelope marked from Juniper & Co.

Elias opened it alone, standing at the kitchen counter.

The cover was exactly as he'd envisioned it: deep gray with a single, subtle ripple pattern in the background, like a disturbance in water. No images. Just his name and the title.

He ran his fingers over it.

Not with pride, exactly.

With stillness.

With care.

Harper walked in moments later, holding a half-peeled orange.

When she saw the book, her eyes lit up.

"Is that it?" she whispered, as if speaking louder might ruin it.

He nodded.

She set the orange down and crossed the room.

Took the book gently from his hands.

Flipped through the first few pages.

Stopped at the one he'd marked.

> I kept thinking I was the ember,
> But I was the page,
> And you were the match.

She closed the book and looked at him, eyes soft.

"This book is going to wreck people," she said.

Elias smirked. "High praise."

Harper shook her head. "No. True praise."

***

The next few days were quiet, but the quiet didn't last.

Juniper & Co. had sent advance copies to literary blogs and indie bookshops, hoping for modest buzz.

But the collection struck a chord.

A reviewer from *The Rookery Review* called it:

"A restrained, gutting meditation on what remains when we stop trying to narrate our grief."

A viral tweet read:

Every poem in Elias Hale's new collection feels like it was written while staring at someone you once loved—and still might.

Within two weeks, Elias was being asked to read in Boston, New York, Minneapolis, San Francisco.

Juniper & Co. offered to sponsor a small, curated national tour.

Just twelve stops.

Poetry cafés.

College campuses.

Indie bookstores with mismatched chairs and too much red wine.

***

Harper was the first to read the offer email.

Elias had left his laptop open and stepped outside to water the lavender.

When he returned, she was waiting at the kitchen table, expression unreadable.

"You got a tour," she said.

He raised an eyebrow.

"You opened my email?"

"I tripped and fell into it."

He chuckled. "And?"

She turned the screen toward him. "They want you in Chicago. Denver. Portland. D.C."

He read it.

Then sat down beside her.

"You okay?" he asked.

She nodded slowly. "Yes. Just… surprised."

"You don't want me to go?"

"No," she said quickly. "That's not it. I'm proud of you. So proud."

He waited.

Then she added, "I just… didn't expect the world to want *you* again. So soon."

Elias reached across the table, took her hand.

"They want the words," he said. "I want *you*. That hasn't changed."

***

Still, the questions began to bubble.

Would she go with him?

Could she, with her own novel approaching completion?

Would they be okay, apart?

Would this... distance them?

She didn't say it aloud.

Neither did he.

But at night, she lay awake longer.

And in the mornings, he made breakfast quieter.

***

One evening, Harper stood on the porch with her phone, reviewing her final chapters.

The novel had taken form.

The coastal archeologist had unearthed a long-lost diary.

A journal full of memories that weren't hers but felt hauntingly familiar.

The story didn't have a grand romance.

It had small moments.

A kindness in a letter.

A mended necklace.

A decision to stay.

She was proud of it.

Terrified of it.

Because it was hers—entirely.

And she wasn't sure if she could let it go yet.

***

Elias stepped outside and wrapped a blanket around her shoulders.

She leaned back into him.

"I think I'm done," she said.

"With the novel?"

She nodded. "Almost. A page or two left. But I know the ending now."

He kissed the crown of her head.

"And?"

"She stays," Harper said. "She doesn't chase the person. She stays in the place. She learns to love herself where she is."

Elias closed his eyes.

"It's perfect."

"I don't know if anyone will read it."

"I will," he said. "Over and over."

***

Elias left on a Tuesday.

The house smelled like cardamom and rain. Harper had baked banana bread, insisting he take half with him on the train.

"People will think I'm the domestic one," he teased, zipping his duffel.

"Let them," she said, handing him a small thermos. "You're very nurturing with a spatula."

They didn't make a scene at the station.

No movie-score kisses. No lingering glances.

Just a quiet, steady hug that lingered a few seconds longer than necessary.

When the train doors closed, Harper waved once.

269

Elias tapped the glass.

Then he was gone.

***

Back at the cottage, the silence was different.

Not lonely.

Not loud.

Just… unaccompanied.

Harper stood in the center of the kitchen that evening, unsure whether to cook for one or simply snack on toast.

She settled on soup.

Made too much out of habit.

Caught herself reaching for a second bowl.

Smiled at the ridiculousness of it—and felt her chest ache in the best possible way.

Love, she realized, was not in the proximity.

It was in the motion.

In the muscle memory of care.

***

Meanwhile, Elias arrived in Boston for his first reading.

The bookstore was cozy and dim, filled with readers who had dog-eared copies of *The Almosts and the After* already stained with notes.

He read with practiced calm.

Until the Q&A.

A young woman raised her hand.

"What's the difference between writing to be heard," she asked, "and writing just because you have something to say?"

Elias paused.

Then said: "I think one is a performance. The other is a promise."

A promise to whom? she asked.

"To the person who writes it," he replied.

And maybe, he added silently, to the one waiting back home.

***

The tour moved quickly.

Boston, New York, Philadelphia.

Then west to Denver.

Elias slept in hotels with too-crisp sheets, drank too many half-cups of lukewarm coffee, and answered the same questions again and again.

But one thing remained constant:

He texted Harper every night at 9:17 p.m.—the time they used to close their laptops and say, "We're done for the day."

She never missed a reply.

Even if all she sent was a note or a heart.

***

Harper, in turn, finished her novel two days after he left.

She typed the final line—just five words:

She stayed. And listened back.

Then sat there, staring at the blinking cursor, until the tears came.

Not because she was sad.

271

Because she hadn't known she needed that ending until it was there.

***

She didn't send the draft to Elias right away.

Instead, she printed it.

Bound it with a single ribbon.

And set it on his pillow.

Waiting.

***

On Elias's sixth stop—Portland—someone handed him a postcard during the signing.

It wasn't fan mail.

It was a message.

No signature.

Just:

You write like someone who's been forgiven.

Keep going.

He held the card for a long moment.

Then tucked it into the inside cover of his own personal copy.

He'd bring it home to Harper.

She'd understand.

***

In Minneapolis, he found a quiet bench overlooking the Mississippi and called her.

"I miss you," he said.

272

She smiled against the phone. "You've only got five more stops."

"That's not what I meant."

Silence.

Then:

"I miss you too."

They didn't say more.

They didn't need to.

Love, they'd learned, didn't always speak in paragraphs.

Sometimes it was just showing up—on time, with honesty, and the willingness to be heard.

***

Elias returned on a Thursday.

The cottage was exactly as he'd left it—lavender sprigs slightly drooped, tea tin refilled, the front path swept clean.

But something felt different the moment he stepped inside.

Not louder.

Not brighter.

Just *settled*.

Like the air had been holding its breath, and now, it exhaled.

Harper was in the kitchen, barefoot and humming a song he didn't recognize. Her hair was up, her cheeks flushed from the oven.

She turned when the door opened and grinned.

"Home?"

He dropped his bag and crossed to her in three long strides.

273

They didn't kiss immediately.

First, they just held each other—forehead to forehead, like they were remembering.

Then Harper whispered, "Welcome back, poet."

And then they kissed.

Soft.

Certain.

***

They spent that evening catching up over dinner.

Harper made her infamous lentil stew.

Elias brought out a bottle of wine someone had gifted him on the tour.

They swapped stories—awkward Q&A moments, surprisingly emotional readings, readers who quoted lines back to Elias with tears in their eyes.

Harper shared the postcard he'd received.

She slipped it into the fridge magnet gallery.

"You were forgiven," she said softly. "You forgave yourself."

He nodded.

"And you?" he asked.

She hesitated, then said, "I finished it."

Elias's eyes lit up.

"You did?"

"I didn't send it because…" she trailed off.

"Because?"

"Because I wanted to watch you read it."

***

Later, she handed him the manuscript, ribbon-bound and printed on thick paper that smelled like fresh ink and courage.

He took it reverently.

Held it in both hands like a keepsake.

Not a product.

Not a proof.

But a part of her.

Harper sat on the couch, blanket across her lap, legs curled under her.

Elias settled into the armchair beside the fireplace.

And read.

***

He didn't speak for over an hour.

Just turned pages slowly.

Let the words sink.

The archeologist's voice was quiet, but firm.

The themes were layered: identity, solitude, inheritance.

No neat resolutions.

Just emotional honesty.

He found himself slowing down, rereading certain lines twice, three times.

By the time he reached the final paragraph, he exhaled—long and low.

Then closed the stack and looked across the room at her.

"She stayed," he said.

Harper nodded.

"She didn't run after love."

"No," Harper replied. "She recognized it in herself."

Elias stood.

Crossed to her.

Knelt in front of the couch and took her hand.

"Then you wrote a masterpiece."

***

She didn't cry.

But her eyes glistened.

Because for once, she believed it.

Not because of reviews.

Not because of future sales.

But because someone who knew her—*really* knew her—saw the book and said, "Yes. This is you."

And liked what he found.

***

The next morning, they sat at the kitchen table with their mugs and talked about what came next.

"Will you publish it?" Elias asked.

"I think I want to," Harper said. "But I don't want a campaign. Or a launch party. Or... a photo shoot in front of the sea."

Elias chuckled. "You mean you don't want to be marketed as *'the real woman behind the story'* again?"

"God, no."

"Then don't be."

She nodded. "Maybe I'll send it to a small press. Maybe I'll just print fifty copies and give them away."

"Whatever you choose," Elias said, "make sure it feels like yours."

She smiled. "I finally know what that means."

***

Outside, the garden was overgrown.

Inside, the kettle whistled again.

They moved like they always did—around each other, with ease.

Elias poured the water.

Harper sliced pears.

No fanfare.

No performance.

Just the quiet return of something rare.

Not the first love.

Not the loud love.

But the *right* love.

The one that stays, and listens back.

***

Harper sent her manuscript to a small publisher in Vermont—a press known for hand-bound books, eco-paper, and authors who kept their day jobs by choice.

No agent. No proposal. No marketing deck.

Just a cover letter, a single email, and the words she had labored over in silence.

They wrote back three days later:

277

We'd be honored to publish your novel.
You've written a story about staying—
and we want to help it linger.

Harper exhaled so deeply she felt her shoulders drop two inches.

It was the yes she hadn't realized she needed.

Not one that said, *This will sell.*

But one that whispered, *We see you.*

***

Meanwhile, Elias received a very different message.

It came from a regional theater company in Chicago.

They wanted to adapt *The Almosts and the After* into a one-act performance—spoken word meets stage play. Minimalist. Intimate.

They'd already highlighted three poems they wanted to center the show around.

The email called it:

> *"An evening of grief, grace, and language we never gave ourselves permission to say aloud."*

Harper found him standing in the garden, the printed email folded in his back pocket.

He held it out to her like a fragile object.

"What do you think?" she asked after reading it twice.

"I think it's beautiful," he said.

"But?"

"But it also scares the hell out of me."

She met his eyes.

"They'll want to know which poems were about me," she said quietly.

"I know."

"They'll want to cast you as a tragic lover."

He smiled faintly. "I've played worse roles."

"And if you say no?"

"They'll adapt it anyway," he said. "Just call it 'inspired by.' You know how this works."

She nodded slowly.

"I want to support it," he added. "I want it to exist. But I don't know if I want to stand under the lights again."

***

That night, they lit a fire outside, the sky bruising violet above them.

Harper pulled her knees to her chest.

Elias leaned back against the deck post, fingers threading through the fringe of the blanket.

"Do you ever miss it?" she asked.

"What?"

"The noise."

He considered it.

"Sometimes," he said. "But mostly I just miss the feeling of *being needed.*"

"You are," she said, without hesitation.

"I know," he replied. "But not by strangers. Not by stages."

She turned toward him.

"I don't want to hold you back."

"You never have."

"But you could be out there again. Touring. Speaking. Performing."

He shook his head.

"I've already performed the hardest role of my life," he said.

"What was that?"

"Letting someone love me after I stopped believing I was worth loving."

***

In the quiet that followed, Harper reached across the gap and took his hand.

"Then maybe the stage isn't where this story belongs anymore."

He squeezed her fingers.

"Maybe the story's already told," he said. "And what's left is the life."

***

A few days later, Elias sent a letter to the theater company.

He declined with gratitude.

Offered to attend rehearsals if they pursued the adaptation independently.

But added this line at the end:

Please remember: this work was born in silence.

Perform it gently.

***

Harper's novel moved quietly through production.

No big rollout.

No pre-orders.

Just a listing on the press's site and a note from the editor:

Sometimes, a story finds you when you've finally stopped chasing one.

They printed 500 copies.

The first run sold out in two weeks.

***

Harper received letters from readers—not many, but meaningful.

One from a woman who said she'd stayed in her small town because of the story.

One from a man who said he now visited the beach to "listen for things instead of collect them."

And one from a bookseller who stocked three copies out of curiosity, then reordered twelve.

Harper read each message with quiet awe.

Not because they validated her.

But because they proved her story had landed.

Not loudly.

But precisely.

***

They didn't throw a launch party.

There were no bookstore balloons, no Instagram livestreams, no champagne popped in a gallery loft downtown.

Instead, they cooked dinner together.

Pan-seared salmon.

Roasted carrots with honey and thyme.

And a bottle of red wine they'd been saving for "someday."

They decided this counted.

***

Elias set the table on the porch—two plates, a beeswax candle, cloth napkins folded just so.

Harper brought out the dishes, warm from the oven, and took a moment to admire the sky.

The sea was calm.

The air held the last of summer's warmth, though fall pressed softly at its edges.

When they sat down, they didn't toast their books.

They toasted each other.

"To the endings we didn't expect," Harper said, clinking her glass against his.

"And the beginnings we didn't plan," Elias replied.

***

For a while, they just ate and watched the sky change.

After the plates were cleared and the candle had burned halfway down, Harper got up and returned with a slim package, wrapped in linen.

She set it in front of Elias.

He raised an eyebrow.

"What's this?"

"Something I've been saving."

He untied the linen and lifted a small, hand-bound book from inside.

The title was pressed in gold:

Stillness Letters

His breath caught.

"These are…?"

Harper nodded. "The letters I wrote you. During the year we weren't sure if we were going to make it."

"You bound them?"

"I wanted to remember who I was when I was still learning how to love you."

He opened the cover, turned a few pages.

Letter Twelve read:

> Today I watched the sun move across the wall in your study.
>
> It reminded me that even stillness has shadows.
>
> But also warmth.
>
> I think I could stay here, even if we never say another word.

He closed the book gently and looked up at her, eyes bright.

"Thank you," he whispered.

She shrugged, suddenly shy.

"I thought maybe we'd make a second volume someday."

He leaned across the table, cupped her cheek.

"We already are."

***

Later that night, they sat by the fire inside.

Not talking.

Just breathing.

Harper curled against him, and Elias rested his chin on her head.

On the coffee table sat their books—*The Almosts and the After*, and Harper's newly released novel, *Where the Wind Leaves Us*.

They didn't look like matching works.

They didn't need to.

They were twin truths.

Born from grief, rebuilt in silence, offered without condition.

No longer stories that needed to be sold.

But stories that had *survived*.

And maybe that was the greatest kind of story there was.

***

Harper tilted her head up.

"Do you ever wonder what people will say about us after we're gone?"

Elias smiled.

"Maybe they'll say we were quiet," he said.

"That we disappeared."

"That we left behind more than we took."

She nodded. "I think I'd be okay with that."

He kissed her temple.

"I'd be proud of it."

***

Outside, the wind moved gently across the porch.

The lavender stirred in the garden.

Inside, two books rested on a table, unstacked—side by side.

And in the quiet between chapters, two people stayed.

Not waiting for applause.

Just *living the story they'd once been afraid to tell.*
Together.

***

The Fire That Remains

It began with a letter, again.

This one printed on thick cardstock with an embossed university seal.

> Dear Harper Bishop and Elias Hale,
>
> We are organizing a symposium at Saint Auguste College on the subject of "Narrative Healing in Modern Literature."
>
> Your respective works—particularly *Ink & Embers*, *The Almosts and the After*, and *Where the Wind Leaves Us*—have been cornerstones of our course for over five years.
>
> We would be honored if you would attend as our keynote guests.
>
> With gratitude and admiration,
>
> Dr. Natalie Saito, Chair, Department of Literature

Harper read it first and left it on Elias's side of the bed, folded neatly beside a note:

> *They want the ghosts.*
> *Do we still have them in us?*

***

They hadn't done a public event in years.

Not since the soft launch of Harper's novel.

Elias had written two more poetry chapbooks in the years since, but both were distributed in limited runs. No tour. No press.

They had grown content with a different kind of rhythm— quiet mornings, long walks, writing that never promised more than it gave.

So when the invitation came, they both hesitated.

Not from fear.

From *choice*.

***

They sat with it for two weeks.

Talked about everything but the letter.

They read together at night, shared meals, tended the garden that had grown into something sprawling and unpredictable.

But the question lingered between them, like steam over a cooling mug: *Should we go back?*

It wasn't about travel.

It was about returning to the past.

To the *story* that had changed their lives—and nearly broken them.

***

On the fifteenth day, Elias stood at the kitchen sink, polishing an old mug that had survived the fire so many years ago.

The porcelain had a hairline crack through the handle, but he kept it anyway.

He ran his thumb across it and said, quietly, "Maybe it's time we told the whole thing."

Harper looked up from the breakfast table.

"You mean publicly?"

"I mean without guarding it."

She hesitated. "It's all in the books."

"Not everything."

She waited.

So he added, "We never talked about what came after. Not really. Not with them."

Harper met his eyes.

Then nodded.

"All right. Let's tell it."

***

Saint Auguste College sat on a red-bricked campus with ivy-covered lecture halls and maple trees that blushed gold in October.

Harper and Elias arrived on a Saturday morning.

Their session was scheduled for Sunday afternoon.

The program listed them as:

"Ink & Embers: A Conversation on Grief, Creation, and the Stories That Save Us."

They met Dr. Saito in a sunlit atrium where students sipped lattes and hunched over well-creased paperbacks.

She was warm, eager, younger than Harper expected.

"I can't tell you what this means," she said, shaking their hands. "We teach your work every spring. Half our creative writing students know *Ink & Embers* better than their own journals."

Harper smiled, a little self-conscious.

Elias just asked, "Do they know how messy it got?"

Dr. Saito grinned. "That's the part they love."

***

That night, Harper reread her original foreword from *Where the Wind Leaves Us*.

The one where she wrote:

> *I used to believe stories were meant to be perfect.*
> *Now I know they're meant to be true.*
> *Even when they're quiet.*
> *Even when they hurt.*

She closed the book.

Elias was reading beside her.

She whispered, "Are you ready to tell them?"

He didn't look up.

But he reached over and took her hand.

And that was enough.

***

The auditorium was smaller than Harper imagined.

Maybe fifty seats.

Wooden chairs. Soft yellow lighting. A single podium up front with a pitcher of water and two mismatched mugs—likely borrowed from the faculty lounge.

Harper and Elias stood behind the podium together.

They hadn't prepared slides.

No quotes.

No rehearsed anecdotes.

Just each other.

And the story they had finally agreed to tell.

***

Dr. Saito introduced them with warm brevity:

"You all know their books.

What you may not know is that their story is its own kind of literature—one built slowly, honestly, and without a guaranteed ending.

Please welcome Harper Bishop and Elias Hale."

Applause rose.

Not thunderous.

But real.

***

Elias stepped forward first.

His voice was calm. Measured. Not rehearsed, but certain.

He looked out at the audience—young writers, professors, readers with notebooks open in their laps—and said:

"I never wanted to be known for a tragedy. But that's where this story starts."

He paused.

"The fire that took my wife wasn't just the end of a marriage. It was the end of who I thought I was."

You could hear a pen drop.

Harper stepped beside him, adding:

"I didn't know Elias when the fire happened. But I read his books long before I met him. They saved me from manuscripts

290

that didn't mean anything—and from a version of myself that kept pretending they did."

Laughter.

Tension released.

Harper continued:

"When I was asked to convince Elias to write again, I thought I was walking into a business deal. I didn't expect grief. Or anger. Or the silence."

Elias smiled faintly. "I didn't expect to say yes."

"But you did," she said.

"I did."

***

They took turns, tracing the arc of their collaboration.

How the cottage had become a studio.

How letters had replaced dialogue.

How every argument became a line in a book neither of them realized was saving their lives.

Elias shared the moment he'd almost quit the manuscript—the morning he threw a draft into the fireplace but couldn't bring himself to strike the match.

Harper spoke of the letter she wrote that same night—the one she never mailed, but later used to write Chapter Twelve.

> *"Love is not the spark," she read aloud. "It's the part that stays when you stop needing to be rescued."*

***

The room was silent.

A woman in the second row wiped her eyes.

A student in the back typed furiously.

Someone whispered, "Damn," under their breath.

***

Then came the Q&A.

A hand rose near the front.

A young man with ink-smudged fingers and a half-tucked flannel asked:

"How did you know it was love—and not just shared pain?"

Elias looked at Harper.

Then back to the audience.

"Because we stopped trying to fix each other," he said. "And started telling the truth."

Harper added, "Pain brought us together. But we stayed for the quiet."

***

Another question: "Do you think healing ever ends?"

Harper answered first.

"I don't know if it ends. I think it... changes shape."

Elias nodded.

"And sometimes," he added, "the shape it takes is a book. Or a morning routine. Or a person who knows when to be silent with you."

***

As the event wound down, Dr. Saito stepped back onstage.

Her voice trembled slightly as she closed the session.

"There are moments," she said, "when literature stops being theory—and becomes a living thing.
Thank you for showing us that stories can burn... and still leave warmth behind."

Applause again.

Longer this time.

Some of the students stood.

Not because it was expected.

Because they'd *felt* something.

Harper squeezed Elias's hand.

They bowed slightly.

Then stepped down from the podium—quietly, together.

***

The campus emptied slowly after the event.

Students drifted back to dorms, professors returned to offices, and the sun dropped behind the main hall's red-brick bell tower.

Harper and Elias didn't head straight to their guest lodging.

Instead, they walked.

No map.

No direction.

Just shadowed pathways, crickets, and the occasional flicker of lamplight against autumn leaves.

Harper held her heels in one hand, bare feet brushing against the cool brick.

Elias carried her scarf, slung over one shoulder like an afterthought.

Neither spoke for a while.

They didn't need to.

***

At the edge of the quad, they found a wrought-iron bench beneath an old elm.

Its arms were carved with initials—some faded, some fresh, love stories waiting for their second act.

Harper sat first.

Elias followed.

She tilted her head back and looked up at the branches, leaves shivering in the soft breeze.

"I forgot what it feels like," she murmured.

"What?"

"To be seen like that."

Elias nodded slowly. "I never liked it."

"I did," Harper admitted. "Once. But tonight… it felt different."

"Different how?"

She turned to him.

"Less like praise. More like… permission."

***

They sat with that for a moment.

Then Harper said, "Do you ever worry that it's already behind us?"

Elias looked at her.

"What is?"

"The work. The relevance. The pages that matter."

294

She didn't say it for pity.

She said it because it had lived, quietly, inside her chest for months.

"I see younger writers now, and I think—God, they're so clear. So bold. I don't know if I could write like that again."

Elias didn't rush to comfort her.

He let the air settle.

Then said, "Maybe they're writing *toward* the fire. We're writing *after* it."

Harper looked down.

Smiled, bittersweet.

"After is lonelier."

"Yes," Elias agreed. "But it's also where things grow."

***

They walked again.

Looped past the library with its arched glass facade.

Passed a fountain choked with leaves and a bike rack still half-full.

Finally, Elias spoke.

"There's something I haven't told you."

Harper raised an eyebrow.

"Am I going to like it?"

"I hope so."

He paused, then said:

"I've been writing something new."

She stopped walking.

"You said you were done."

"I thought I was."

"And now?"

"I think I have one more in me."

She crossed her arms, teasing. "Is this a sequel to *The Almosts and the After*?"

"No," he said. "This one's about staying."

***

They sat again—this time on the library steps.

Elias reached into his coat pocket and pulled out a folded sheet of notebook paper.

Not typed.

Not edited.

Just ink and instinct.

He handed it to her without a word.

Harper opened it.

Read:

> I was never looking for a muse.
>
> Just someone who wouldn't flinch when I set my story down, still smoldering.
>
> You didn't flinch.
>
> You read the ashes like scripture.
>
> You stayed.

She looked up.

Eyes glassy.

"You wrote this for me?"

He nodded.

"I'm calling the collection *The Fire That Remains*."

***

They sat there long after the night had fully settled, students passing like shadows in the distance, lights flickering on in dorm windows like stars.

Two authors.

Two people.

Not writing for acclaim anymore.

Not waiting for awards.

Just sharing pages that felt like home.

And in that quiet corner of the campus, beneath trees older than their grief, they felt something like beginning again.

Not because they had to.

But because they could.

**

They met the students in a seminar room with low ceilings and a circle of battered armchairs.

No podiums.

No PowerPoints.

Just faces.

Open, eager, uncertain.

Five undergraduate writers. Two graduate fellows. A teaching assistant with calloused fingertips from guitar strings.

Dr. Saito sat on the windowsill, notebook closed, letting the room breathe without her steering it.

Elias sat with one ankle over his knee, casual but focused.

Harper curled sideways into her chair, like she did at home when reading a new manuscript—alert but comfortable.

**

The first question came quickly.

"How do you know when something's *ready*?" asked a girl with dyed-blue hair and a sleeve of literary tattoos.

Harper smiled gently.

"You don't," she said. "You just stop being afraid of what it might say about you."

Elias added, "Sometimes I don't know it's ready until someone else reads it and says, 'Yes. That's how it feels.'"

Nods around the room.

Pens scribbled the words down like commandments.

***

Another question.

"Have you ever written something that scared you?"

Elias laughed softly. "Almost everything I've published scared me."

Harper nodded. "If it doesn't scare me, I wonder if it's true."

A boy in the back, tall and quiet, said: "Your books helped me talk to my dad again. After my mom died."

Silence followed.

The kind of silence that felt holy.

"Thank you," Harper said softly.

Elias didn't speak.

He just looked at the boy and nodded.

As if to say, *We know.*

***

Another girl asked, "What happens when you feel like you're writing the same story over and over again?"

Harper leaned forward.

"Maybe you are," she said. "But that doesn't mean it's wrong. It just means you haven't reached the ending yet."

***

The conversation lasted over two hours.

They didn't talk about marketing, or plot points, or industry trends.

They talked about *grief that didn't make sense* and *love that didn't arrive on time*.

About being told their voices were too quiet, their stories too soft.

About writing, not to change the world, but to *not disappear inside it*.

***

Afterward, the students lingered.

One asked for a photo. Another asked for a hug.

Harper gave both.

Then they were alone again, the room echoing with what had just been shared.

Elias stood by the window, gazing out over the leaf-strewn quad.

"They don't need more critics," he said.

Harper tilted her head. "What do you mean?"

"They need someone who remembers what it felt like to write in the dark."

She crossed to him. "You mean…?"

"I think we should teach," he said. "Not full-time. Nothing official. But maybe… a workshop. A retreat. Something small."

Harper was quiet for a moment.

"I never saw myself as a teacher," she admitted.

"You already are."

She looked up at him.

He smiled.

"You just didn't know your students yet."

***

That night, back in their guest quarters, Harper pulled out her journal and wrote two words at the top of the page:

The Rewrite.

Below it, she scribbled:

> A writing retreat for stories still on fire.
>
> For voices too soft to be sold.
>
> For people who stayed anyway.

She looked across the room.

Elias was asleep already.

Peaceful.

As if nothing in the world needed to be proven anymore.

And maybe, she thought, that was true.

Maybe they didn't have to publish more.

Or speak louder.

Maybe the real legacy was not what they'd written.

But what they were ready to pass on.

***

The train ride home was quiet.

Elias read an old Wendell Berry essay.

Harper sketched a rough logo for *The Rewrite* in the corner of her notebook—a spiral notebook filled with loose ideas, annotated with half-sentences like:

- "Stories that arrive late are still worth telling."
- "One cabin, ten chairs, no WiFi."
- "Acceptance letters written by hand."

They didn't speak much during the ride.

But every few minutes, one would glance at the other and smile.

The kind of smile that said: *Yes. We're doing this.*

***

Back at the cottage, the lavender had begun to dry.

Autumn was arriving slowly, creeping in with gold-tipped leaves and cooler mornings.

Harper opened all the windows.

Elias brewed chai from scratch, grounding the space again in warmth and ritual.

They didn't rush back to their desks.

They wandered.

Walked the garden.

Noticed small things.

The way a spiderweb had strung itself between the rosemary and the trellis.

The way the light hit the windows at 4:07 p.m. in October.

And when they were ready, they began to build something new.

***

The Rewrite was never designed for scale.
Just one retreat.
Ten writers.
Seven days.
One coast.
They found a small house for rent on the northern edge of Maine—whitewashed wood, large windows, a path to the sea.
No tech packages.
No brand partners.
Just notebooks, conversation, and a kitchen that smelled like cumin and sea salt.

***

Harper wrote the invitation letter by hand.
Then typed it up.
It read:

> *We're not offering a breakthrough.*
> *We're offering a pause.*
> *For writers who've forgotten what it feels like to write without an audience.*
> *For stories written at midnight, but never shared.*
> *For those who carry grief like rhythm and still believe language is holy.*
> *Come sit with us.*
> *We'll keep the kettle on.*

—Harper & Elias

***

They received nearly 300 inquiries.

They chose ten.

Some were published.

Most were not.

One had never shared her writing with anyone.

One was revising a manuscript rejected fifteen times.

One wrote poetry on the backs of receipts.

They arrived quietly.

Anxiously.

Harper and Elias greeted each of them with tea, hand-written name cards, and a small pebble placed on each bed.

"Your story," Harper explained, "is still heavy enough to hold."

***

By day, they wrote in silence.

By night, they read aloud.

Not for critique.

But for witness.

And in the gentle cadence of shared words and firelight, a kind of healing emerged—not performative, not polished, but *earned*.

***

On the sixth evening, one participant—a quiet man in his sixties—read a poem he'd written about his late wife.

When he finished, no one clapped.

303

But everyone leaned in, as if closer might mean safer.

Elias nodded slowly.

Then said, "Thank you for giving that shape."

And Harper, beside him, added, "Thank you for not waiting until it was perfect."

***

When the retreat ended, there were tears.

Long hugs.

Letters tucked into journals.

No promises of publication.

Just something deeper: the permission to continue.

To write even if no one asked you to.

To stay, even when the plot was unclear.

To tell the story, simply because it wanted to be heard.

***

Back at the cottage, Harper and Elias unpacked slowly.

Ten letters from the attendees waited on their kitchen table.

One included a line that neither of them forgot:

You taught us how to write from the fire, not about it.

Elias framed the note.

Hung it in the study.

Right beside the postcard he'd received on tour years ago:

You write like someone who's been forgiven.

And beside that, Harper pinned a fresh slip of paper, newly written, just three lines:

The ember is not the end.

It's what stays warm.

Even in the quiet.

***

The Last Line

The title came first.

Before the words. Before the structure. Before either of them knew what it would become.

Harper had jotted it in the margin of a to-do list while cleaning out a drawer.

She showed it to Elias at breakfast, sliding the paper across the table between slices of toast.

Ink & Embers.

He smiled.

"That's it," he said.

Just like that.

No debate.

No questions.

Because sometimes, after everything, a title *wasn't* just a name.

It was a home.

***

They didn't plan for it to be a book, at first.

It began with letters.

Mostly ones they'd never sent.

Journal entries.

Annotations.

A poem Harper had written on a napkin at a cafe in Vermont that began:

> I used to believe the fire would come back.

Now I light candles.

Elias had dozens of fragments.

Some typed, some scribbled on the backs of receipts, some pulled from the margins of manuscripts he thought he'd abandoned.

Harper began to collect them in a file.

One night, she printed everything they had and laid the pages across the living room floor, building a kind of constellation—memories orbiting a shared center.

They stood over the mess of pages and looked at each other.

"This isn't a book," Elias said.

Harper agreed.

"But it might be a map."

***

Over the next few months, they shaped the fragments into something intentional.

Not chronological.

Not clean.

Just real.

Some pages were dated.

Some weren't.

Some entries were only three lines long.

Others stretched for pages, winding like long walks toward understanding.

They called it a hybrid.

Not memoir.

Not poetry.

Not correspondence.

Something in between.

Like their story had always been.

***

Harper wrote a preface.

It read:

> This is not the story of how we fell in love.
>
> This is the story of how we stayed.
>
> *It is not polished. It is not clean.*
>
> *It is not fiction.*
>
> *But it is honest.*
>
> *And it is ours.*

They printed that on the first page—no dedication, no acknowledgements, no ISBN.

They weren't publishing it for bookstores.

They weren't selling it.

Just printing a small batch for people who'd walked alongside their story.

And those still learning to stay with their own.

***

They mailed the first copy to Dr. Saito.

Another to each of the original *Rewrite* attendees.

One to the young man who'd once said he talked to his father again because of *Ink & Embers*.

And a handful more to people they'd never met in person, but who had sent letters years before. Whispers of gratitude and grief and resonance.

Inside each copy, Harper slipped a small card.

> You don't need to finish the story to be part of it.
> You just need to stay.
> —H & E

***

One afternoon, Elias walked into the study and found Harper reading through an early draft of her first manuscript—the one she'd nearly trashed before meeting him.

She looked up at him and smiled.

"I thought this version was garbage," she said.

"It was," he teased, and she threw a pencil at him.

They laughed.

Then she added, "But it wasn't without fire. Just no one to help me name it."

Elias knelt beside her chair.

"We name it now," he said softly.

"Together."

***

That evening, they hosted a small gathering in their garden.

Ten chairs.

String lights across the fence.

Tea, wine, bread, olives.

And a basket of books.

Not for sale.

Just to be taken.

No one needed to ask what they were.

People knew.

This was *that* kind of story.

The kind you only found if you were ready.

***

The shoebox had been buried under years of manuscript pages and notecards, long forgotten in the back of Harper's office closet.

She found it while looking for spare printer ink.

Inside: old correspondence.

Paperclipped notes.

Editorial memos from her early days at Grange House.

But in the middle of the stack was a plain white envelope with her name typed neatly on the front.

No return address.

Inside was a printed manuscript excerpt.

Chapter One of *The Ocean Doesn't Ask*.

No cover letter.

No context.

Just margin notes in blue ink.

And on the final page, a single handwritten line:

> *Tell me if it's worth finishing.*

Harper blinked down at it, stunned.

She hadn't seen that page in over a decade.

Elias walked in, carrying two mugs of coffee.

"What did you find?"

She held up the letter.

He took it, turned it over, and chuckled softly.

"I remember this," he said.

"I didn't," she whispered. "Not fully."

"You were the first person to read anything I wrote after Camille died."

"I almost didn't respond."

"You almost didn't stay."

She looked up at him, blinking back the sudden ache in her throat.

"But I did."

"You did."

He sat beside her on the floor.

They read the old chapter together.

It was raw. Wandering. Full of unanchored grief.

The writing had grown since then.

But the voice—his voice—was already there.

Searching. Honest. Trying.

She touched the last line again.

"Do you think you were really asking if it was worth finishing?" she asked.

Elias shook his head slowly.

"I think I was asking if *I* was."

***

Later that evening, Harper dug out her old laptop—the clunky silver one with the missing "F" key.

She scrolled through a folder titled "Queries."

Thousands of them.

Rejected, responded to, archived.

Near the bottom, she found the original email from her assistant.

Subject: Unsolicited submission—author in Maine

Just read this. You're going to hate it. It's messy. Pretentious. But there's something in here I can't shake.

Should I pass or respond?

Harper had written back only one line:

Don't pass. Ask him what happens next.

She read it aloud to Elias now.

He smiled.

"You never asked that again."

"I never had to," she said. "You kept answering."

***

They talked late into the night.

Not about the books.

But about the spaces between them.

The parts of their story that had nothing to do with plot.

The early mornings in the kitchen.

The rain on the porch during editing marathons.

The argument about chapter order that turned into a breakthrough—and a kiss.

How Harper had once deleted three full pages of Elias's work and he hadn't spoken to her for two hours.

How he later admitted she'd been right.

And how neither of them had any idea what they were building—not really.

Not then.

"We could've missed it," Harper said quietly.

Elias nodded. "We almost did."

She leaned her head on his shoulder.

"What would've happened if we never met?"

Elias traced a finger along the spine of the book beside them.

"Maybe we'd still be writing," he said. "But we wouldn't have been *seen*."

***

That night, Harper couldn't sleep.

Not from restlessness—but from fullness.

From the realization that this wasn't just a story about survival.

It was a story about being *witnessed*.

And how rare it was to be truly read—by someone who doesn't edit out your worst moments.

By someone who stays through them.

***

In the early hours, Harper tiptoed back to her desk and wrote a letter—not to Elias, but to the woman she'd been when they met.

She didn't plan to send it anywhere.

It was enough just to write it.

You didn't know if you could do this.

You were angry, and brilliant, and tired.

You thought stories were only valuable if someone else said so.

But someday, the story will be yours.

Not the one you sell.

The one you live.

Keep going. Even when the pages don't make sense yet.

Especially then.

***

The invitation went out by postcard, like always.

No RSVP link.

Just a handwritten note:

> Come if you're ready to listen.

> Come if you're still carrying the match.

Ten former retreat attendees returned.

Each had grown since their last visit.

A few had published.

One had started a grief-writing group at her community library.

Another—quiet, once unsure—was now teaching creative writing to teenagers at a school tucked between two cornfields.

They arrived not as guests.

But as kin.

***

The garden had changed, too.

The lavender was gone now, replaced by low pines and wild roses.

The gravel walk had been widened.

Elias had built benches from reclaimed wood, tucked beneath hanging lanterns that glowed amber as twilight approached.

Harper hung a sign on the side of the old writing shed:

Tonight: One Reading Only.
Ink & Embers.
No books for sale.
No sign-up sheets.
No introductions.

***

The group gathered just after dusk.

Ten chairs circled around a small fire pit.

A stack of hand-bound copies sat in the center like a sacred offering.

No one touched them yet.

Not until the words had been spoken.

Harper sat beside Elias, hands resting gently on the pages.

She looked around the circle.

Faces illuminated by firelight.

Soft. Honest. Open.

And then she began.

***

"There are stories we write because we're trying to leave something behind.

And there are stories we write because we finally stayed."

Her voice didn't rise.

It didn't need to.

Elias picked up the thread.

"This is not a story of redemption.

It's a story of permission.

To stop performing.

To stop apologizing."

They read alternating passages.

Letters, lines of poetry, fragments of reflection.

Some pages felt like echoes.

Some like brand-new wounds finally softening into skin.

**

Halfway through, Harper read a passage written the day after Elias had walked out of a meeting with his former editor, refusing to monetize the fire:

"He didn't say a word on the walk home.

But when I handed him the draft, he didn't ask what was missing.

He asked if I wanted tea.

That's when I knew: this man would never make me earn love again."

No one moved.

No one interrupted.

A few people wiped tears silently.

One attendee reached for the hand of the writer beside her, and neither of them let go for the rest of the reading.

**

Elias read the final entry.

Just a paragraph.

One page.

The last page of *Ink & Embers*.

His voice steady. Clear. Like the air had been waiting for this:

> "We kept calling it a story.
>
> But it was always a fire.
>
> It burned through the life we thought we needed— and left behind the one we built with what remained."

Silence.

Then breath.

Then stillness again.

No applause.

Just shared presence.

***

Harper closed the book gently.

Then spoke, not from the page, but from herself.

"People asked us, over and over again, when we knew it was love," she said.

"I think it was when we stopped needing each other to be brilliant.

When we became... readable.

Even in the margins."

Elias added, "And when we stopped trying to write the perfect ending."

Someone asked quietly, "So this is the last story?"

Elias smiled.

"No," he said. "But it's the last one we needed to explain."

***

Afterward, they handed out the copies.

No names inside.

No preface this time.

Just pages.

And trust.

Each person who received one held it like a warmth between palms.

Not a book.

Not even a gift.

A recognition.

***

Later, around the remains of the fire, Harper looked out over the flickering shadows of people she'd once only known through insecurity, doubt, or silence.

Now they were here.

Holding their own stories a little closer.

Not because someone had told them they were worthy.

But because they *remembered*.

***

Autumn arrived in full.

The garden quieted, save for the rustling of leaves that never quite let go until winter insisted.

Harper moved slower now.

Not because of age, exactly.

But because stillness had finally found its place in her body.

She didn't feel pulled by deadlines anymore.

Or pages waiting to be filled.

Instead, she'd wake, drink tea by the window, and *listen*.

To the wind.

To the sea.

To her own breath.

Sometimes she wrote.

Most days, she didn't.

***

Elias had taken to archiving.

Old notebooks, letters, and early drafts filled boxes labeled with years instead of titles.

He bought a scanner.

Taught himself how to digitize everything without rushing it.

Harper teased him—called him "the literary museum curator of our past."

He didn't deny it.

Some things deserved preservation.

Even the mess.

***

One evening, while sorting through old correspondence, Elias found a page Harper had written in the margin of a rejection letter she'd never sent.

A simple line, circled three times:

"Maybe this was never supposed to be big.
Maybe it was supposed to be honest."

He left the page on her desk.

Harper read it in the morning, and cried without shame.

Because that sentence—written in frustration, years ago—had become a truth she now lived by.

***

They stopped giving interviews.

Stopped answering emails from publishers wanting sequels, adaptations, "legacy collections."

Elias joked that someone once pitched a television series called *Embers & Ink* where they'd be fictionalized as "troubled artists turned literary detectives."

They laughed about it for weeks.

Not because it was ridiculous.

But because it reminded them: the real story had never been the plot.

It was the process.

The staying.

The slow burn of becoming.

***

Harper turned down another invitation to keynote.

This one was from a major conference.

A flattering offer.

Full travel.

Honorarium.

A panel with "literary greats."

She turned to Elias after reading it aloud and said, "They think we still want to be known."

He smiled gently. "They don't understand."

Harper nodded. "We already are. Where it matters."

***

Still, they weren't disappearing.

They mentored quietly.

Met with small groups of writers at the retreat once a season.

Read first drafts.

Encouraged edits made with care, not fear.

Elias began writing letters again—real ones.

Handwritten.

To strangers who left notes in the guest book.

To former students.

To one reader who had sent him a message eight years earlier and said:

> Your poems don't fix me.

> But they keep me company while I try.

He wrote her back.

Said:

> *That's all they were ever meant to do.*

***

They weren't avoiding legacy.

They were *rewriting* it.

Not as something made of applause or awards.

But as something made of echoes.

Quiet affirmations that the story had landed.

Not loudly.

But precisely.

***

In the evenings, Harper would sometimes reread old chapters—not for edits.

Just to remember.

Not the words.

But the woman who had written them.

How she once doubted every sentence.

And how, somewhere between ash and ink, she had started believing in her own voice.

Not because someone else told her to.

But because *she'd stayed long enough to hear it clearly.*

***

Elias, in turn, worked on a final poetry collection.

It was untitled.

Untimed.

He added a line here and there.

Sometimes weeks apart.

It wasn't a book, exactly.

More like a weathered notebook he tucked under his pillow.

Not for readers.

Not for Harper.

Just for himself.

To keep warm.

322

***

The bookshop was tucked into the corner of a narrow seaside street, just beyond a fishmonger and a frame shop.

They hadn't meant to stop.

They were on their way home from a short weekend trip— one of those little escapes where nothing was scheduled except sleep, old records, and pastries from a town they didn't know well.

Harper spotted the window first.

A small display of weathered titles and handwritten recommendation cards.

Inside: wooden shelves, uneven floors, and a smell that could only be described as *time and ink*.

It felt familiar.

Not nostalgic.

Just *true*.

***

Elias wandered toward the poetry section.

Harper made her way to a low display table stacked with journals, small-press chapbooks, and zines.

And there, in the center, was a copy of *Ink & Embers*.

Hand-bound.

No barcode.

A note tucked inside the front cover, handwritten in soft graphite:

Donated anonymously.

This book stayed with me when nothing else did.

Pass it on, if you're ready.

Harper blinked, stunned.

She reached out and touched the cover like it might vanish.

Elias appeared behind her, saw the book, and smiled.

He didn't say anything.

Just placed a hand on the small of her back.

***

The shopkeeper noticed them looking and walked over.

Mid-thirties. Denim apron. Smudge of ink on their wrist.

"Beautiful book, that one," they said. "Not for sale though. We've had five people try to buy it. But it's part of the free shelf now. You can read it here. Or take it and bring it back."

Harper opened her mouth.

Then closed it.

She didn't say, *We wrote it.*

She just smiled and asked, "Do many people read it?"

The shopkeeper nodded.

"All the time. Sometimes they just sit with it for an hour and cry. One person copied an entire poem into their journal last month."

They paused.

"You know it?"

Harper looked at Elias.

Then back at the shopkeeper.

"Yes," she said. "It's been with me for a long time."

***

They stayed in the shop for almost an hour.

Didn't buy anything.

Didn't need to.

Harper left a note in the back of *Ink & Embers*, hidden behind the last page.

Just a few words, scrawled in her familiar script:

> *Thank you for staying.*
> —H

She folded the page back into place and set the book down gently.

And then they walked out, fingers entwined, the bell on the door offering one soft chime as they stepped into the afternoon light.

***

The drive home was quiet.

The kind of quiet that doesn't need filling.

Elias kept one hand on the wheel, the other resting palm-up between them, where Harper's fingers laced through his.

At one point, she looked out the window and said, "I used to think love needed to be loud to matter."

"And now?" he asked.

She smiled.

"Now I think the stories that whisper last longer."

***

Back at the cottage, the season was beginning to shift again.

Not dramatically.

Just enough to notice.

A leaf here.

A chill in the air there.

Harper opened the windows.

Elias lit the fire.

They sat together on the couch, each with a book—one written by neither of them.

They didn't talk about writing.

Or readers.

Or the future.

Just sat.

Present.

Together.

***

On the mantle sat three objects:

A small wooden box of matches, untouched.

A lavender sprig from their original garden, long dried.

And a single framed line from *Ink & Embers*:

> "This is not the end.
> This is the last line before we begin again."

***